ZAP

Confessions of a Channel Changer

*A novel? Yeah, sure.
Why not?*

Simon P

*Manuscript released by
Dr. Heinrich Gautier*

ZAP: Confessions of a channel changer

ISBN: 978-0-9878711-6-9

Copyright © 2012 by Dr. Heinrich Gautier

Published by Dr. Heinrich Gautier

PROLOGUE

I may be criticised by some colleagues for releasing the journal Simon P, my patient for a matter of weeks, kept while under-going short-term intensive non-interventionist therapy at the Lilac Hills Institute in Natenpeg, Ontario, Canada. But that is a risk I am prepared to take because I believe it is vital that other psychiatrists, psychologists, therapists, counsellors and social workers learn from all that transpired during the time that Simon P was under my intensive non-interventionist care.

I want others to see firsthand how, given little more than a self-appropriate medium and minimal guidance, clients can use intensive non-interventionist therapy to jolt themselves out of memory lapses, denial and psychological barriers that inhibit the process of self-understanding, and can then move forward into the process of self-discovery and self-awareness and, in an ideal world, self-healing.

Yes, there is a degree of intervention with the intensive non-interventionist therapy process; however, as you will be able to judge by Simon's journal, it is minima—often nothing more than setting up the process and being present in the room in latter sessions until the patient chooses to leave and, it is hoped, carry on the process in other environments. Although, as you will come to understand, I now see that there are opportunities for mild yet constructive intervention in the non-interventionist therapy process. In fact, there may be times when this is desirable.

With that in mind, I believe the intensive non-interventionist therapy process clearly demonstrates that what causes a patient to choose to remember is as important as what causes a patient to choose to repress, and that what causes a patient to chose to remember must come from within if the patient is to experience the delta factor or tipping point, i.e. if substantive change is to occur. However, one may, based on the case study (for that is what this journal is, an intensive non-interventionist therapy case study), want to judiciously moderate the degree of non-interventionism to produce optimum results. We learn from infancy—ours and those of any therapy. So this is to be expected in any therapy *nouveau,* like finding the optimum thermostat setting for a furnace *nouveau.* As these sessions demonstrate, however, the intervention may be little more than being there. On the other hand, and this may reflect my early childhood behavioural therapy practice, like Goldilocks we may try several interventionist dishes—but just a taste of each—before we find one that is just right.

To demonstrate the intensive non-interventionist therapy process, and to enable you to follow Simon P's process of discovery, I have chosen to publish the journal of Simon P in its entirety, using the title he scribbled on the cover of his journal. Some is fact, some is fiction. Some we cannot tell. That's not the point. It's where Simon goes, or perhaps should I say where the therapeutic process takes him. And it takes him close to where he wants to be, or needs to be, or should be or could be. I confess, I am not sure anymore. But in my doubt, I find certainty. In certainty, I find little more than arrogance, so I welcome my doubt, the doubt the process, and Simon's subsequent actions, infused me with. Welcome and embrace the uncertainty as it means my work is not yet done.

With that in mind, I think it fair to say that this journal graphically demonstrates the altered states that Simon P experienced during the writing-therapy and his involvement in, and process through, intensive non-interventionist therapy. But I will not attempt to label his states on your behalf. That is something you must divine here if you are to practice intensive non-interventionist therapy with any of your patients, if the College of Psychologists of Canada reinstates the public practice— as I am hoping the publication of this journal will encourage them to do.

Ultimately, one must pose this question: Was the therapy a success? I will not debate the question here, although my scientific opinion is clear, even though I admit to some uncertainty. Ultimately, though, I will allow you to judge.

As for me, I now use intensive non-interventionist therapy in private practice not governed by the College. I am, as therapist, tasting various bowls of porridge, so to speak, and non-intensively intervene sooner in the process as may be required. And if non-intensive intervention by an intensive, non-interventionist therapist sounds like an oxymoron, so be it. Therapy is, after all, a process—for the patient and the therapist.

Note: I have, for the most part, not altered spelling, punctuation, grammar, verb tense or any inconsistencies in Simon's journal. I have revised as minimally as possible a few passages where interpreting what Simon P referred to as 'jerky handwriting' proved to be difficult. I have also changed names and locations to protect the innocent, although one might say I have protected those not yet found guilty in some instances. And I've replaced the section dividers Simon P used, which tended to be images of skulls, penises, testicles, breasts, and ink stains blotches, with three asterisks.

With that, I have said more than I intended to say, and have said it a little more intensely. So let me not intervene any further in your process and allow me to present you Simon P's journal, *ZAP: Confessions of a Channel Changer*.

Dr. Heinrich Gautier
Director, Psychiatric Services (former)
Lilac Hills Institute
Natenpeg, Ontario, Canada

DAY THE 1st

Goat seems content to talk—give me a few mundane instructions and ask me a few even more mundane questions, as if I'm an idiot who does not understand the obvious: I'm fucked; this assignment sucks—and let me sit silently. As if he thought i was thinking about my response to him. ha! Although he asked me if there was anything at all i wanted to say before we, or at least I, got started on this idiot assignment, project or whatever the fuck he called it. Therapy? Sure. Shit. Which is why he got no reply at all.

'well,' Goat says, after talking at me for a while, asking the usual questions & trying to conduct the usual tests—setting up the process, about two weeks, he says—and not getting any feedback. 'I want you to write for me,' he said to me. 'Write about anything. You know, just jot down stuff & see what comes up. How would you feel about that?'

Just like that he says it, as if he's not after anything in particular. He even hands me a green spiral-bound note book & a pen. a BiC. Writes first time it does i discover as i scribble on my hand to show Goat i'm rebellious but not daft—i know what write is.

At one point he mumbled something about being entirely honest with oneself over the next two weeks or so as a good place to start.

As if.

'well,' Goat says. 'Before we meet 2morrow,' he says, 'i'd like you to try it. I hope you give it a shot ...'

Why should i try anything, i don't say. A shot? Shoot him, maybe. Sure if I had a gun or a hammer, I'd hammer in the morning, all over this place ... . I know were maxwell keeps his silver hammer ...

'Well,' Goat says, 'i guess that's it then.'

Just like that. that's it then. That's. it. then. And I'm on my own. On my pursuit of the character Me a name I call myself—the ellusive prey—until whenever. Until I am found and it is finished.Untill it is done or I am well done.

And just like that, I'm back in my room, then in the common area watching the glorious orb—a Tv or not tV—then the dining room, long before dinner praying for manna to fall from heaven. I'M HUNGRY. To no avail ...

* * *

Like i said, i didn't give him any feedback so i didn't ask him why i should try it. i'm not talking. haven't talked for how long? since before the trial.

the trial, ha. a monkey zoo. a show trial that.

i'm not talking. i've got to remember this 2morrow too. Goat is swift, but not as cunning as me.

& maybe i shouldn't be writing either. but then i've only taken a vow of silence. & writing doesn't break the silence. Besides, i'm not going to show Goat any of this, unless i want to: my choice. & besides besides, i've got fuck-all else to do. to-dah. too-dumb.

* * *

6

silence. my choice. because nobody has ever understood before. i won't give them a chance any more. why would i? they still wouldn't understand. like Goat who i was sitting in front of a few minutes/hours/days ago—(what does time matter, i'm madder than a hatter)—his grey hair, little Goatee, & granny glasses protecting his tired eyes: probing/asking; doing his job— like hitler's SS, generals and soldiers. why would he understand? why should he understand? end of the day, he has a life—goes home to his wife to his wife to his wife ...

*　*　*

If you want, you can write me your dreams, Goat said.

dreams. Ha. I have no dreams to dream. but, as an adolescent, i often dreamt of falling—falling from great heights & never hitting the ground.

Sometimes i'd climb to the top of the slide at Sunnyside Pool & then, rather than slide down into the pool, i'd fall off the ladder towards the water.

The fall. so dangerous & yet so sensual. as i fell, a warm breeze massaged my body in waves. oh how i wished i could fall forever. & then the surface, so close. How i struggled to wake before i hit the surface. & if i had hit? What then? would i have plunged below the surface, a prisoner of dreams no more?

i don't even know what the fuck that means. it means i was a coward, afraid to hit the surface. even now, afraid to plunge beneath the waves ...

*　*　*

7

yes, i can write if i want to because he doesn't have to ever see any of this. or maybe, if all goes well, he will see all of this. (if everything goes well? like hell. when has anything ever gone well.) he'll never see everything there is even if he sees everything i write the songs that make the whole world sing ...

if all goes well, this writing could just be my ticket out of here.

right Goat? write?

what is there to go well? what is there to understand? what is there to get out of? what is there to get into if i were to get outta here?

* * *

Goat actually says to me: 'there's no need to talk if you don't want to share your voice with me, Simon. just write. i understand you used to write a lot.' (he's flipping thru a file as he says this. & i don't say, Come on Goat, get it together: do your homework before you call in the client.)

'might i have seen some of your stuff on Tv?' he says. 'Any particular commercials i might remember?'

sneaky Goat. i almost say something but i catch myself ... Shit, he's swift, this Goat is. But i've outrun swifter.

even though i'm tempted to tell him ... but i remember my vow & bite the tip of my tongue. Draw blood. Open my mouth & answer him with my blood.

'Right,' says Goat. Or was it, Write? 'After all, you are a writer.'

ha, writer. don't know how that can be said with a straight face. i used to be an advertising copy writer. &

he has the audacity to call me a writer? Fuck, Goat, thou hast a sense of humour.

'take your time. put it all down,' he says, '& we'll see what floats to the surface. you may want to talk about that. it's up to you. all of this is up to you.'

* * *

up to me, eh Goat? take my time, eh Goat? like you've got all the time in the world; that's what i've got. you leave here at night. you go home to your wife. you've got a life. me, i've got got got my time... i've got you babe; i had you babe. i've had you babes.

* * *

'all of this is up to you,' he says. as if it's my idea to be here in the first place. & fat chance, anyway, me writing about anything i refuse to talk about. write indeed.

* * *

i'll write for now, until i get hold of the channel ZAPper LARD-ass controls in the common room. Then i'll have something more meaningful to do dah do dah ... until then, with fuck-all to do dah do dah, i'll write the blood of an english man ...

i'll write it down what floats up in the green notebook Goat gave me with this BiC pen he gave me. but i'll be damned if i'm showing him anything 2morrow, or ever and ever and ever and a day. not showing it to him at all, not any of it. i'm sure as hell not talking about it. not that there is anything to talk about.

But what is this? i already wrote that down, didn't i? didn't i blow your mind this time, didn't i? didn't i turn you on, babe, didn't i? didn't i?

unless, of course, it's what's gonna get me out of here— this writing down what floats up—then maybe just maybe baby, i will ... write for Goat? talk to Goat? talk, no! silence got me here. it'll get me out, if there's any getting out. it sure as hell kept me out of there, where i'd be some thug's déjà vu bum-boy. or worse. living in isolation with the real assholes of the universe only a yelp away.

Hey, i read the news 2day, oh boy. i know what's locked up on the other side. the side where i am not because i'm not one of them, Goat. silence kept me out from where they are, where i don't wanna be… which is one of mine: *be what you wanna be.* you may have heard it sung on Tv by a heavenly host milk toast milk toast.

not that here is any cup of tea. not that i have socialites for company. like LARD-ass who controls the channel ZAPper ergo the Tv in the common room. You'd think in a government-run institution there'd be some semblance of democracy! maybe i ought to file a human right complaint. Or an inhumane rights one, two, three, what are we fighting four don't ask me i don't give a damn…

*   *   *

… but if per chance writing & talking are my tickets out of here ...

*   *   *

i'm not your man i said when they hauled me in. & they slapped me down & i knew then that silence was my

only weapon. the silence that has protected me all my
life. the silence that you want me to break—that you
want to break ...

silence protects me, not that i have anything to confess.
the evidence was fabricated. the witnesses all lied. & the
all-female jury went along for the ride ...

and to think, one time i could've been the champion copy
writer of the world ...

* * *

'you used to be writer,' Goat says thumbing thru my files.
'An advertising copy writer.'

he says that & does not smirk. nice guy. then he looks
over his granny glasses and peers at me as if i'm
supposed to beg forgiveness for it. shit-head. i shrug my
shoulders & he strokes his little billy-Goat gruff Goatee
of a beard.

put it all down & see what floats up.

* * *

hey. look at me. i'm floating. bull.

* * *

he knows i used to write copy, but does he know that i've
put it down before? how can he know that? it can't be in
my files. or does it say this there about me:

as a child simon hid in the closet of his mind & wrote
there in invisible pencil where nobody could see what he
had to say. he lived in the lead-poisoned closet of his
mind & wrote on the backs of coats & on the souls of
boots & shoes. & he scribbled with his fingertips on the

11

pages of the billy bee corn syrup notebooks his mother got him when she bought billy bee corn syrup. then he tore up the pages & flushed the images he had created down the toilet.

& the toilet overflowed. & he was given more to write about.

& as the child grew, he ate & ate pancakes smothered in corn syrup so mother would have to buy a new bottle of syrup almost every week so he could get new notebooks to write in. to write friends he did not have. to write the family he did not have. to write about the angels who brought him anything he wanted & took him anywhere he wanted to go—mostly to make-beleaf gardens to watch johnny bower & the Toronto make-beleafs defeat the dreaded canadiens ...

*   *   *

who was all that about? me? or somebody other who i don't know any more. i don't know.

is all that in his file?

and even so & even so. so even if i had a vivid imagination & a boring childhood. even so.

*   *   *

and what if i write for you Goat & nothing floats? what if my feet are made of lead & they hold me under? what if i go down to retrieve my stuff & the weight of it all holds me under? what if i go down once, go down twice, go down three times? what then Goat? who will save me then?

because i've never been down before, down below the surface ... where there is nothing but absence of light. Nothing, as if. as if there is anything to explore.

there is me. & i am here.

i AM WHAT FLOATED UP. i am. therefore iamwhatiam. What floated up i am.

* * *

this is poker. is he bluffing? write it down is all i really have to do? (That's mine too: *all you really wanna do, you can do with <delete product placement>.*

perhaps though that's it: if nothing floats up, there's nothing there. & if there's nothing there, then i'm outta here.

yes. my ticket outta here. nothing. that's my ticket outta here. just gotta keep it all under control as i put it all down, without lies or deception. Yes. The Truth the whole truth & nothing but the truth, so help me. Goat shall set thee free, & my confessions. the truth shall set thee free. the pen, my ticket outta here, mightier than... i shall wield it like a sword and slay mine enemies.

right Goat? maybe you & this silly game. my tickets out of here.

* * *

hey, i gotta go. Family Ties is on. at least it's on if i can wrestle ownership of the channel ZAPper away from LARD-ass , that donkey who looks like he's been here forever & is gonna be here forever more. Him i can handle. & you too, Goat. You too. now that i know that nothing must float up—& nothing will float up because there is nothing to float up.

But maybe i'll leave LARD-ass for later. when there's not so many of his cronies around—his disciples on the couch & on the chairs & on the floor. what an ass. but he holds the ZAPper in his hands. & they worship him. slobber for him.

perhaps i'll just hide out here in my cell of a room. for a while & we'll see what comes up, eh Goat?

here, watch this come up.

*   *   *

damn orderlies.

hey, jerks, i was just following orders! to see what comes up. all i did was stick my finger down my throat. Goat would be proud of me, digging so deep so soon.

damn orderlies don't understand a thing. they need more training in human relations. instead of tossing me in the shower 'cause i puked all over myself, they should empathize with me. don't they know don't they know don't they know?

*   *   *

but now that i've been scrubbed clean of my sins, let me handle this. let me man-handle this. this thing i can flick but not write with—or can i flick this in one hand & write with the BiC in the other?

dear Goat,

please excuse the jerky hand writing... Ha ha ha... zzzzzzzzzzzzzzzzzzzzz......

14

* * *

ah, once again, man-handled. nectar of the gods in the palm of my hand. but i'd prefer to worship in front of the Tv. is wrestling on? what day is it, what time is it? there must be wrestling on. but LARDass & his loonies won't vacate the Tv set.

Tv or not Tv? either way, it's something i prefer to do alone. like making love. (Love? Ha! Ha ha ha… zzzzzzzzzzzzzzzzzzzz……)

where's the social convener? there must be something else for these dudes to do. something more for me too ...

LARDass i'll handle in the fullness of time. but can i handle you ...

... oh god, where did YOU come from? your black hair combed back in thick waves. Black except for a bermuda triangle patch of grey at the back of your head ... That much i remember about you. That. & the day you disappeared.

What i saw when YOU went out the door was the back of your head—the triangle streaming out of the door like a storm cloud about to burst. so long ago, it was, wasn't it? at least your lifetime ago it was, wasn't it?

& then another lifetime ago when i got a phone call from the lady who said 'your father's dying.' & i said: *Good*. & she said 'That's not very nice.' & i said: *He wasn't very nice*. She said: 'He's changed.' & i said: *Death does that to people*. & she said: 'He wants to see you.' & i said nothing. but i took down the address. And I took what I could get, and when she looked at me with her big brown eyes… aye.

& when i came to see you, out of curiosity not sympathy, i was shocked to see that you had sunk beneath the triangle: where dark waves once crashed there was a lake of grey & white. & you didn't recognize me—but for the first time, ever I saw your face, i looked into your eyes. Under the yellow film i saw a hint of green. Your eyes were green once, like the sea. Like the sea. like mine eyes.

& i was sick, sick, sick. Sea sick.

& the lady said: 'get him out of here. i can't take care of him. i don't want to take care of him. i never wanted to take care of him. i'm too old to take care of him. besides, you were right about him. He isn't very nice. take him away.'

And i was sick sea sick all over.

'Shit,' the lady said. 'You're as bad as he is.'

And i fled. Because. it is, was, would soon be, finished.

* * *

& that night i dreamt of the sea. Of drowning in the sea. A sailor went to sea sea sea to see what he could see see see and all it was he saw saw saw was the stormy sea sea sea ... & i went under once. i went under twice. i looked for your hand to hold on to, but no hand was offered. i went under 3 times and never resurfaced.

i dreamt of old rugged crosses. carrying three rugged crosses into a cave. erecting the crosses in the darkness. crucifying me myself & i on the crosses. & shadows. it bonfires beneath my feet and i was consumed by flames ...

& i woke up with my pecker in my hand and sperm all over my belly. & i knew that the king was dead. & i wondered if the king would ever live again.

* * *

well, that was a good run, wasn't it Goat? that ought to be worth a few brownie points? hey, if i keep this up, i ought to be outta hear in a day or a week or a year or two.

* * *

& when i got home, she had candles & steak & flowers & was radiant, she was. & she hugged me & said: 'simon, i'm pregnant.'

just like that: *simon, i'm pregnant.* what was i supposed to do, father, as YOU lay dying in some flea-bitten flop house? what was i supposed to do as i began to understand that i was me & me was you & that that would be the dance of intimacy between us forever & a day? that's what made me puking sick in your room— that realization. & what was i supposed to do?

so i hit her.

& i fled for the second time that day. as i had fled time after time. even though i had thought, for a brief moment—oh candle in the wind—that i might never have to flee again.

* * *

jesus wept. simon fled.

to the home he had once, so long ago, known. and he crawled in thru the basement window unprotected by any silver spoons in his mouth… and wrapped himself up in old newspapers and rags, and dreamt of stormy seas and old rugged crosses ...

* * *

you see, Goat, what came up?

having fun? as you try to roll away the stone that covers my heart. what if you succeed & find not an empty tomb but a corpse? what then? what then? what then? what, pray tell, then?

but this is nothing new. you know all this shit. it's in the files. you could just look it up. why make me write it down? why keep me up past the midnight hour doing this when i could be watching the late show, looking at knockers on the blue movie channel, jerking off to the phosphorous angels that dance on the Tv screen ...

... i'm gonna wait for the midnight hour, until my loves comes ... Ha! Love never comes. to get love, you gotta rip somebody off. in the midnight hour.

* * *

i met her at the ad agency. we could talk. Why? i don't know. perhaps i was into proving for a season that i could be as others were. (but for what reason?) & we became friends, then confidants ... At least she learned to confide in me. & i allowed myself to listen. & then we became ... lovers. in a dangerous time. But she didn't know how dangerous the times were.

the times they are changing. shit-heads stay the same.

She showed me her scars & bruises. But i didn't scar or bruise her ... until the day she said ...

18

but i never let her see me, until that day so who was braver?

one day, before all that, she told me that she had started to dream about me. in my dreams, she said: you're my knight in shining armour. you save me from fire-breathing dragons ...

And she described the dragons & what they tried to do to her. all familiar, the dragons were. i have known such dragons in my life. but this i didn't tell her. i was once such a dragon. but this i didn't say as i became a drag on her.

i had lost my voice even then—the voice i never had.

& she didn't recognize me as a dragon. she thought i was st. george. Me. HA!

& i embraced her & felt no urge to breathe fire upon her & then ... me ... discovered that me ... loved.

& then the lady called. & i watched my father as he lay dying. & when i got home, my lover told me she was pregnant & i became the dragon of her dreams—i hit her... I ... slashed her... belly. She knew. She knew. She must've known this would happen to her and what had happened to others ... women know the facts but don't want them spelled out. In the dark they'd rather stay, right mother other ther er r.........

*　*　*

oh how my belly aches from all this belly aching. but still none of this is new, is it Goat? all of this you knew, didn't you Goat. it's all in my files, isn't it?

*　*　*

you know, i've never had a wet dream since. or a dry one cum to think of it. i've never given myself the opportunity. i masturbate more often than daily. i spill & spill my seed until i'm drained & then i sleep but never dream, wet or otherwise

* * *

am i asleep & writing in my dreams? or am i awake & dreaming of sleep writing?

if awake, i will sleep. even as i write.

Right. Write. Right… i'm back. Aren't you glad i am? don't you wish everybody was?

* * *

i once had a lover whose name was Ted. Hey-nonney-nonney-oh. He caught AiDS & now he's dead. Hey-nonney-nonney-oh.

i left ted, long before he got AiDS. He was no fun. i'd say do it, & he'd do it & then some.

i am not homo or hetero. i am carnal. libidinous.

My sideburns. ted loved my sideburns. oh what sideburns i had. Mutton-chops, we called them. Tight curls running from the top of my ears to the side of my chin. Like a face full of pubic hair. Ha!

But, oh, that was long ago. i was so much younger then. i'm older than that now.

he would've held on to me, but i had to let go. & now he's dead, is ted.

* * *

Sometimes i wonder, as if it matters, will i die of cancer? i feel like the kind of creep who should, you know. A long painful death that could've been prevented if only it hadn't been misdiagnosed. Or perhaps in a bloody car accident, just live long enough to realize my head's been severed & is sitting on top of the world or in my lap. perhaps my head won't know it's dead, & it will go down on me ...

& i, in an accident without clean underwear.

Or will my heart attack? Or Big Mac attack? Or Iraq attack? Or will i go blind? will i wear my trousers rolled?

will some lone stranger in a washroom somewhere bite my pecker off just for a lark. in the park. in the dark.

& the morality squad has it all on video tape 'cause they know the joint's a cruising place & they had it under surveillance. & they'll sell the tape to Snuff Films inc. & make a small fortune on my small thing, dangling between some old farts dentures.

Thank god for Poly Grip! What a grip. Get a grip.........

*   *   *

you'll wonder where the yellow went when you brush your teeth with pepsodent

*   *   *

Things could be better. They could be worse. i could be you, reading this.

*   *   *

Someone left the cake out in the rain. i don't think that i can take it. Cause it took so long to bake it. & ill never have that recipe again. Oh no ...

Here comes the rain again, falling on my head like ...

Rain drops keep falling on my head ...

And i wonder, still i wonder, who'll stop the rain ...

*   *   *

Yes in the early days, i would feel so fucking guilty every time i masturbated. But then i'd go to church. To church i'd go. To the serious house on serious earth where I'd be filled with the spirit. The holy spirit. The all-forgiving spirit to whom i would confess my sins. so simple really. ask for forgiveness & it is granted. tah-dah. & jesus would love me once again. & the fix would last, oh, until about the next sunday night. & i'd go back to church & confess my sins all over again & i'd be born again again. & i'd be clean again. & jesus would love me over & over again.

*   *   *

There was only one fear, that i would die before i woke & on the magnitude of my sins i would choke. But soon i got over the fear. & once i was fearless, i didn't even need the fix of forgiveness.

There. i confessed. i'm a sinner.

Now Goat, let me the fuck out of here!

And into where? Or underwear. Or over there. Or.

*   *   *

22

i'm worried Goat. you see, last night, before we met i actually had a dream. the first dream i can ever remember having since the waves & cave ... i'm worried that i might be getting weak, letting my guard down. is that the case, ace?

in this dream, two kids were fighting on the lawn in front of a house down the street from the house i grew up in. i was walking by & saw the fight. One kid was getting the worst of it so i interceded. From out of the house came a bigger kid—bigger than the two kids fighting. Bigger than me: the size of Frankenstein. He lumbered down the stairs & ordered the kids to start fighting again. To the death, he howled.

Then he turned to me & kicked me, hard, in the nuts.

i crawled home & puked in my backyard, in my mother's vegetable garden & her tomatoes started to grow & grow & swell & swell & swell & burst & i passed out only to be wakened by two kids butt-fucking me, not taking turns but (butt) together, as Frankenstein stood over us & laughed, hooted & howled at the full moon...

* * *

Fuck it. i'm tired. Oh so tired. Too tired for this game. Lame game. Take aim at this game which is lame... oh lord, how i wanna go home. I wanna go home. I feel so fucked up, I just wanna go home.... But you tell me this is home. No. This is hell. i should've let them stone me. Stone me to my soul. Stone me like a jelly-roll.

it's hell inside this head, i tell you. & you don't care. you've imprisoned me here. i can repent & repent all i want, but there is no one there to hear. There is no one to grant forgiveness.

& that, goat, is hell.

And that, goat says, is it. I can go… but not home, no. to my room. Tomorrow we shall do it all again. Me writing, him saying next to nothing. 'yes.' 'carry on.' 'and then what.' Shit like that, without even looking at my scribbles, my illegible scribbles, which I don't have to read to him or show him, he says… so, what the fuck is the point, I don't ask.

Tomorrow, then, he says. And I am escorted back to my hole in the cave of this mountain of a place….

Wait, is this a try, a reply? depends i guess on whether he gets it or not. and even if he gets it, will he get it?

and yet here it is: i'm trying. or is he trying me? Hmmmmm … Either way, he's got me going … will have to put an end to that, soon. Sooner than later. Soon.

DAY TOO

what time am i supposed to see you 2day, Goat? have i got time for this?

i hate honesty, which is what you're asking for. but i'll never tell you that i hate honesty. & i'll be damned if i tell you why. Honestly.

*   *   *

ah, Goat. if you could read my mind. you're sitting there looking all perplexed, nattering at me. you can see i've written. you can see me writing thru your talk. you can see i'm doing what you want me to do. but you can't see that i won't confess. because i have nothing to confess to.

it's actually dull stuff, Goat. would make you yawn. But hey, did you know that the brain chemical that causes a man to get an erection also causes him to yawn—that's been my life, one yawn after the other.

but i'd wish you'd shut up. i'm trying to write.

here, watch me ignore you totally.

*   *   *

yesterday, after i saw you Goat, i sat in at the back of the common room: the room full of common twits. like what's wrong with this picture? who does not belong here? me! but of course. Mais oui. Oui oui oui all the oui home…

they sat in front of it, the Tv the Tv the Tv, they did. LardAss controlled the channel changer. the ZAPper. a

25

ZAPper a ZAPper... my kingdom (cum) for a ZAPper. i figure he got it, el ZAPper, either for good behaviour or because he's such a lard-ass nobody is gonna challenge him. except me.

because if there is a Tv & a ZAPper, then i control the ZAPper. it has always been that way; will always be that way. Now and forever, amen... ah, men... ah. men.

except these guys are prime ZAP-outs. zombie ZAPs. you don't just walk up to them & deal with them in a reasonable manner. no. if you stood between them & the Tv, they'd looked around you, or through you. that's what happened when i got up & stood in front of them. Then LardAss ordered a couple of them to knock me outta his line of sight. but i figured he wasn't gonna fight me & that his wusses would crumble the moment i made a fist. so, i simply grabbed the ZAPper out of fat man's fat hands. as simple as that.

or so i thought.

until the beast tackled me as i made for a spot on another sofa. he knocked me to the ground, pinned me on my back, lifted his hospital whites—oh, god protect me he ain't got no underwear on—and sat full force, hole force, dark fucking shit hole force, on my face—until the orderlies came. I swear they hesitated before they pulled his hole force off me. I swear.

i thought they would haul him away, but they didn't. they removed the ZAPper from my hands, gave it to the man mountain who got up without a struggle & headed back to his spot on the couch. & all his ZAP-happy side-kicks sat in front of Tv as he resumed channel ZAPping.

he was lucky i didn't bite his balls off. no underwear & i swear he hadn't bathed for weeks. the stench was so foul, i couldn't catch my breath to bite his balls off. Butt I will one day bit his balls off given the opportunity knocking at my door, do me a favour and let him in…

* * *

i must confess, i am tempted to show you this, Goat. i suspect you'd see the unfairness of it all. or perhaps you'd laff. but if i gave it to you, that would be like me talking to you, wouldn't it?

What am i asking you for? you can't hear a word i'm putting down, never mind what floats up. the lord is my shepherd, i shall not talk. to talk would be to concede that i exist on the level of these ... animals, minerals, vegetables here. which is no doubt what you think, because you've tossed me into the same room with them ...

get me outta here! or i'll get me outta here. trust me, i will. & i'll be damned if i'll play the game your way. i'll show such an abstract work of art that you'll think it should be hanging in a gallery. a gallery, Goat. do you read me? only you won't get to read me or hear me.

* * *

Now he's through with the preliminaries, the platitudes & the mumbo-jumbo probing & he's asking me how i feel, as if he expects me to tell him. Feel. ha. Feel this…

* * *

here's something i'm sure you'd love to hear or read. Slobber for it. the dream i had last night. all Goats love dreams. Aye, Goat, ye are not me first.

i was driving a car which was coated in Noxzema. i drove it into a subway station, down the escalator & into the tunnel. A train came chasing after me. i drove as fast as i could but the Noxzema meant the car kept on slipping off the tracks. i gained control of the vehicle just as i went around a long, sweeping curve & saw, at the end of the tunnel, a light. Of another train coming at me. head on ...

make of that, what will you?

*   *   *

& then i dreamt that i walked up behind my mother when she was looking into the refrigerator, bent over trying to get something off one of the lower shelves. i shoved her into the freezer, swiping her vagina as I shut the door. as she suffocated, i masturbated with her cunt.

make of that, what will you?

*   *   *

do you want to share any of your work with me? Goat asks. i hate the s-word. And the f-word. Feel, not fuck, but of course.

i wouldn't share this with him any more than lard-ass would share the ZAPper with me. (oh, the stench of that man's ass coming down to meet my face. The agony, the agony… the memory scares me still.)

*   *   *

i think i'm wearing down Goat. but what's this he's saying
...

he says: 'i won't see you for 12 days. i'm glad you
decided to start writing. i hope you keep it up. when we
meet again, you can share your writing or your voice
with me. over the next 12 days there may be times you
wish to see me—that won't be possible. i don't want to
intervene in the process you've started. it's an important
process. i think you know that. so i hope you continue to
write.'

i cap my pen. or i will, as soon as Goat stops talk

*   *   *

ah, this is better. away from Goat. back in my room. i've
just de-cap-itated my BIC. i'm not going to write much. &
if you think i'm gonna write for two weeks, you're ...
 wrong. write? & as for wanting to see you—HA! why
would i?

*   *   *

& after he said what he said, there we were. a stare
contest—sharing the silence. but sharing no thoughts or
words. I cap my pen and shove it in my shirt pocket and
finally he blinks. he says: 'good. this is progress.' just like
that: 'this is progress.' no sarcasm. not even a hint of it.
as if he's actually content.

'keep it up,' he says: 'get it down. whatever comes up.
even the lies. & the dreams. you'll get a long stretch
now. but i suspect you have a lot to go over.'

he says: 'anything else before you go.'

i shake my head.

(SHIT i SHOOK MY HEAD. i COMMUNICATED!)

he says: 'good.' & nods towards the door.

asshole. slippery slimy beast.

IN THE MEANTIME …

i have two black eyes. i've sprained my wrist—my right wrist, not my write wrist. Or should I say my wrist has been sprained.

i'm going cold turkey on Tv. i swear i will never approach the mean man-mountain for the ZAPper again.

i've confined myself to my room, even if the orderlies think that they've confined me here. i'm not gonna leave, not for two weeks, until it's time to see Goat again. I'm gonna conserve my strength & then punch that son-of-a-bitch's lights out. putting me in this hole without Tv. Tv or no Tv, i'm gonna punch out his lights. and i'll do it without saying a word.

* * *

i don't have to do anything here, for the next two weeks. not even this. but i do this for me, not for Goat or freedom. what else can i do to pass time? pass gas? piss off? what else what else what else? Same as those on the outside. We are all passing time. Time keeps on passing passing…

i wonder sometimes if i will ever see freedom. sometimes i wonder if they want me to wonder if i will ever be free. & sometimes i wonder if i've ever been free …

there's no reason to keep me here. none of those zombies in the common room is capable of this: i challenge any of them to string together more than two inarticulate grunts.

they can imprison my body with these rats, but they cannot take my heart, my soul. no. my mind is mine.

* * *

see, Goat, your tactics aren't working. Nothing comes up any more. you thought you could handle me. well, nobody could ever handle me.

i must admit, when first i met you, i thought we might work together on a scheme to spring me. i thought if you proved your worth to me that i would play your game in return for my freedom. but now i know, you're just a prison guard without a gun. you're a torturer without a whip.

how many lashes was my sentence?

insanity indeed.

who's insane, the man who does not want to serve his sentence or the man who services me here by keeping me locked up here? Really, if I didn't wanna get out of here it would be a sure sign of insanity.

i write only because there is nothing else to do. all my life i have done what i have done because there has been nothing else to do. people have done things to me because they have had nothing better to do. that's as best as i can figure it.

go figure it ...

* * *

my lip is swollen. lard-ass really laced into me. i refused stitches. i've tasted my blood. it reminds me that i'm alive. but i forgot how bitter life tasted.

yes, i have tasted my I've tasted the blood-soaked selfishness of cosmic proportions inflicted upon me. more often than i care to admit. but i have not tasted my blood in a long, long time. how bitter i forgot ...

am i bitter about being here? it's comfortable, yes, three squares a day, better than anything I'd ever cook up — food, not schemes. but It would be even more comfortable if i could forget that i bleed, that I'm alive. It would be more comfortable if i were dead. or watching Tv. My programs on Tv or not Tv. That is the question: will I ever get to watch my Tv.

they want. a confession, or my death.

they can't have either. they're not gonna get me. it's why i'm here, Goat. i'm the one the authorities came to blame. they tried to get my confession, i told them nothing, not even lies. so they bent me in an effort to break me. but i refused to break.

all my life i have bent. but i've never broken. & you will not break me. i will sit back, write, eat. i will be as comfortable as i can be.

Goat, you blew it. i am no longer in a hurry to leave this place 'cause I be comfortable, which means this writing goes nowhere & you get nothing. not a word you can use against me. & when all is written down and when i am ready to leave, on my terms, in my way, i will hand it over to you, & you will find nothing in this writing to keep me here ...

* * *

here's something for you, Goat:

we, each of us, carry within us, the secret meaning of the universe. so if you can unlock the key to me you will unlock the key to mystery. believe it. And suck on it.

i was going to write out my philosophy in life. it's not worth the effort, my philosophy in life.

in case you missed it, Goat, that is my philosophy in life: it's not worth the effort.

* * *

don't want to talk about the weather. don't want to talk about a girl named Trudy. I got to know her well. well, i didn't. it wasn't worth the effort. she thought she knew me well. she made the effort. see where effort got her.

* * *

this is not worth the effort.

But it is a bigger effort to not do this, to simply be in this place as time passes pisses pusses. as this place remains in place ...

oh Goat, get me outta here ... get the man-mountain off my face.

* * *

something is supposed to happen 2day. what? i can't remember or think of anything in particular. where's my day planner? It was here a minute ago ...

shit, wrong place, wrong year, wrong life ...

* * *

I ate my young because they shit themselves. there. How's that for seeing what floats up. except, i had no young. i left home when i was young. i left my lover before she had a young. i ate no young. i had no young to eat.

* * *

i miss beer. i can hear a beer commercial on Tv in the lounge—the Blue Jays are losing to the Tigers, again. here, there is no beer. i get no buzz. i can't get no buzzifaction.

remember *buzzifaction* for Queen Bee honey? that was my campaign. You know the one, the pooh-type bear romping through the woods singing *i can't get no buzzifaction. But i try. Yes i try ...* then the queen bee comes on screen & says seductively *you want to get a little buzzifaction, honey?* ... cut to Queen Bee honey. Damn, I was good. I was good and damned. But I was good, honey, wasn't I good? But yes, I've been bad. Baaaad... ha. It's all subjective, ain't it. Good, bad, indifferent... all subjective.

i want get a buzz. Can't get a buzz with the cheap drugs they serve here. i want a buzz. to keep me quiet. to end this flow.

Yes, i've been bad, subjectively speaking. No surprises. after all, i'm here. there must be a reason. have i committed treason?

Through the door & down the hall i can hear its call. The siren's song. the Tv set. now that would be something to dull the dullness of the absence of buzz. but LardAss guards the channel ZAPper. & the hoard around the set, they will not let me have it & i've been unable to take it from him. did i swear off another attack? i did? so since when have i ever made a promise that i've kept.

remember, i used to be an ad man ...

it's all that quells the angry beast: Tv.

LardAss i can handle. i will handle him without a trace. Get him the fuck off my face. Outta my head. Into my bed...

*   *   *

Argh, it's getting worse, the blood I taste... I mean it was like 'okay blue jays, let's get balled.' That be the slogan, no? which is exactly what i tried to get. What do you expect without buzz or a Tv i can call my own? Besides, she had tits like a cow, the nurse did. i just wanted to milk them.

so i said to her: Let me milk your tits, please.

Goddamnitall, i said: please.

Uniforms are sooooo sexy on woman, starch on top and wildness below ... thighs flying high and skirts inch up (how fucking far can they go?) while the cap, the nurses cap, stays primly put. Talk about your oxen and morons! Prim and proper and looking like bear in the woods in mating season ... shit in the woods, the last thought I had, or might have had if I had thoughts, before my orderly friends arrived too soon. now i have a fat lip & bruised cheek to match my black eyes. they'll probably tell Goat too. well good, damnit, it might get me there sooner—it's a lot more exciting sitting there saying nothing & writing than it is sitting alone in my room saying nothing & writing even les.

ah, but it worked, even if i paid in blood & bruises. they've given me a stronger buzz. and now to sleep ... zzzzzzzzzzzzzzzzzzzzzz,,,,,,

*   *   *

like all good buzzes, this too has passed. But how long has passed. That's what it's all about, shake it all about, and pass… pass time, pass out, pass the ball, pass on it, piss on it… pass.

*   *   *

oh to be Tv & write poetry for the lonely heart, the sacred heart, the solitary tree, the bumble bee that stings me.

oh moon. oh sweet rhapsody in blue. Is it true that we do what we must do? but when is it the last time that you & i did screw?

i can feel your breasts against my naked chest. i inhale. exhale. i can feel your heart beat. be still my beating heart. 2 hearts beat as 1, like buddy rich on the drums. the blood runs so red to my face. so jazz cool you are. so like mellow marshmallow tit willow ...

& there, your belly ... now it too is beating. but 3 hearts cannot be 1, no—ono: john&yoko. & in the end, all you have is the end. & there is no such thing as a unified trinity. that much i know. and this too i know: it was time for me to go & leave beating heart(s) behind.

& you had experience brutality before. or so you said. & as i left: déjà vu, no doubt you said. say, did i tell you about my lover, ted. ted is dead.

* * *

and where did it leave me, what i did?

jobless. homeless. & roaming the streets.

so i started with the street where i grew up, where i threw up nights in the closet where i hid when the fee-fi-foe-fum giant stalked the earth.

that's where i went. only nobody was home. of course not—the giant is dead.

& nobody lives there any more. not even alice who could make herself as little as ... did she ever grow up? how could she ever grow up?

my kingdom. my non-existent kingdom for a magic mushroom.

* * *

ah, but the streets are full of vipers who have magic mushrooms to sell. so go ask any alex masquerading as alice—you know she'll understand that logic don't mean a damn thing at all when you're ten-feet small ...

* * *

so i moved into the house (more like a dilapidated cardboard box on a small gravel lot). i squatted in the space/place on the street where i grew up because it was familiar & comfortable ... & besides, it was available, with a hammer to break window to slither through. & besides, nobody was home. not even memories.

and i got drunk & i got high & i bought a Tv & illegally hooked up cable ...

& it all came back to me to me now: the street smarts
you had developed before you went back to school &
then settled into work & done real good at yer copy
writing too ... & then you fell in love, & 2 hearts beat as
1, but then fell outta love when 3 hearts made it crowded
house ... mini and mickey mouse with rat, not where it's
at.

& i set up house-keeping in the house where i grew up
on the street where i grew up in the places where i
screwed up.

right? go ask alice. do you think she'll understand? not a
hope in hell. she don't understand fuck all.

*   *   *

there's no place like home, right dorothy. thank god,
dorothy. what would i do with another place like home ...

*   *   *

what the heck. i'm perplexed. about the complex sex
we're making. i'm faking. he/she is talking. nobody is
talking, except those who are talking at me. i can't hear a
word they're saying. it's like they're braying, stubborn
asses, at the dark side of the moon ...

*   *   *

relationships. i've had a few. & they didn't seem all that
hard to do. it's like anybody you pass in the street is
suitable, even if they avert their eyes the first time they
pass you by. just say, hi. they're not expecting it. & if
they think you're weird, smile & you tell them that you
are & they relax. because they're vulnerable. everybody

is vulnerable to the person who smiles when he says hello.

* * *

suffer the little children to come unto me before i come into them ...

* * *

Goat, this isn't funny any more ...

* * *

it's time to go ZAP channels, only LardAss still rules the couch. besides, i've confined myself to solitary confinement. & i don't fancy a dirty hairy ass in my face again. or his hairy knuckles in my eyes again ...

* * *

2 weeks more, minus however many days it's been. & then another & another & another ... how many more? 4 dead in Ohio. how many more?

* * *

& everybody you pass in the street, you kind of wonder if they look at you & go home to beat their meat or even give you a second thought. imagine it, all the possibilities that we deny each other every day when we pass in the street & do not say so much as hello. Hello in there, hello.

* * *

Remember this: *Imagine The Possibilities*. my greatest campaign ever. sold i forget how many million whatevers.

imagine the possibilities. you heard-it-here first.

so eager we are to imagine the possibilities of anything
& everything but each other ...

*   *   *

When Goat had me in his office on DayTOO (seems like
last week – month – year – decade – life time – universal
time) all he did was talk a little & smile a little. & said:
'maybe after writing for 2 weeks, you'll be ready ... '

i'll never be ready. doesn't he understand. isn't he paid
to understand?

damnit, fight me Goat. nobody ever asked me for
nothing. they just took what they could get & when they
looked into my big green eyes, they said you ain't seen
nothing yet & they took even more.

it's the only way to get anything from me: take it. oh i'll
fight you for it, but i'll lose. i'll lose.

*   *   *

like when she looked at me with those big brown eyes &
said, 'i'm preg…'

*   *   *

'& we'll get together in 2 weeks,' Goat says. & that's all
there is to it. & i'm left alone with ... my… words.

Words. Sometimes I love them, I admit. More often I
hate them. Sometimes I manipulate them. More often
they exploit me. Sometimes I befriend them. More often
they betray me. Sometimes I use them. More often they
abuse me. Sometimes I open my mouth and hear no
words—hear nothing but the rasping sound of air
struggling to escape my constricted throat. Sometimes I
put pen to paper and watch pen sit there waiting for

words to occur. Sometimes I put pen to paper and watch it race about like a headless chicken leaving unintelligible stains on my page. Words. Sometimes all of this happens. Sometimes none of this happens. Sometimes I reject words ... More often more often sadly more often ... words reject me.

*   *   *

& i'm back in the house where i grew up & there's not a fucking thing that i can remember.

nothing. you hear me?

*   *   *

i was walking in woods lost & anxious when i came upon a well-travelled path that took me some place i did not want to go & found myself wishing i could be walking in woods lost & anxious ...

*   *   *

All of this & my inquisitioner ain't even here to inquisition me. 2 weeks? fuck him. does he really expect me to keep this up? a steady diet of this for 2 weeks. he'll see me in 2 weeks? he said 'start at the beginning or the end or the middle or anywhere you want & put it down, put it all down.' there are many i put down.

'Write it down, write it all down as if you were a ship wreck & see what floats to the surface. & then, if you want, you can share it with me or not. eventually, it all floats to the surface, or washes ashore,' or so he says.

hey, i want to say, nice metaphor. but you know fuck all about ship wrecks. sometimes what goes down stays down. remember the titanic?

41

2 weeks of this i cannot stand. In the corner I will stand, and pass my time away, pass away in the corner I will stand and pass...

DAY the THIRD

My grade two teacher's name was Mrs. Marshall, poor dear.

'Mrs. Marshal is a marshal, she'll shoot you down like this: Bang! Bang!'

I sang that song about Mrs. Marshall, made it up right on the spot, as a friend of mine was sipping his Coke during lunch hour. Poor kid. He laughed so hard, he snorted the Coke out his nose which caused me to laugh so hard I pissed my pants, which caused him to laugh so hard he started to choke and then turned blue and if Mrs. Marshall hadn't been on yard duty he might've died but she came by and rescued him by giving him mouth to mouth and--after he recuperated--we laughed about how he had kissed the famous marshal, Mrs. Marshall ... 'Smooch smooch!'

*   *   *

i had a dream last night that i slipped out of my room before lights out—and skulked down the corridor to Goat's office. i left this ... writing ... outside his office (i couldn't fit the notebook under the door).

at least i thought it was a dream. this morning one of the orderlies returned it to me. just dropped it on the edge of my bed as I was getting up. he said not a word, but grinned ...

i've got to be stronger than that... now, off to see the Goat...

* * *

trust is important, Goat. you've got to trust me.
Especially when i say that i've nothing to confess. i didn't
talk thruout my trial because i had nothing to say. the
evidence against me was fabricated. the witnesses. in
collusion, all lied. somebody wanted to put me away &
the all-female jury went along for the ride.

when the deck is stacked against you, every word you
say is twisted & distorted & thrown back in your face. i
know Goat, i've been there before.

i had nothing to say, even if i seemed to have confessed
to the contrary here. i can't hear a word i'm saying. only
the echoes of my mind. & i'm not sure i believe a word
i'm saying anyway. It all seems ... unbelievable. (yawn.
Oh gawd I'm boring myself to death here... maybe that's
the way to go...)

i know i'm here now, but anything before here ... dunno.
dunno. & now it's your job to get at the truth. but it's got
to come from me, eh? ain't no way around this is there?
okay, i'll give you what you want, no more.

any more than you need, that may float up, i'll erase.
Save it for another day, a darker day, when the getting
out doesn't seem as easy.

* * *

write about it. as if there's anything to write about. you
forget, i used to be an advertising copy writer. i can
make you buy anything, Goat. but that's okay, because i
can see it in your eyes—buy my innocence—it's what
you want to do. & because you want it, my subliminal
seduction will work.

this is not subliminal, you say, because i'm telling you about it? ah, but this is the most insidious form of subliminal seduction—when the seduction is masked under the revelation that the seduction is apparent. trust me. i know. you don't. i can tell. & i bless you for it, your innocence.

but i need you, if i'm gonna do this for me, Goat ... oh i need you. i need you, my lord—if i'm gonna get outta here.

all together now: woke up. Got outta bed. Dragged a comb across my head. came unstuck in time & space. There's an alien on my face ...

*   *   *

the dream! last night's dream.

and alien upon my face. he wore a white nightie. his genitals looked like the inside of a cave, you know with those things that hang down or hang up—i could never keep them straight—stalagmites & uptights. & on the wall of his genital cave, a shadow show—the creation: from chaos to garden, in 6 days, then he rested and the snake slithered into the scene, and the rested was history.

And when the show was over, he let me up to breath. He was a little man with circles of glass around his green eyes. A Goat-like beard hangs from his chin. & like everybody i know, he talked at me. That was okay. i couldn't hear a word he said. i had my head on reverb & i was lost in the echoes of my mind.

*   *   *

45

yesterday, this was such an easy game to play. that was before they put me away. oh hell, i don't even remember my yester-daze.

* * *

i wonder wonder who, who, who wrote the book of inquisitions?

i mean, i don't understand how you could just sit there as i say/said nothing. It was almost effective though. there were times i nearly burst—the voices in my head wanted to come out & parachute into you shouting *geranium* ...
 but i said nothing & you kept me seated there, giving me opportunities to not answer your questions.

Doesn't he know, i have no answers to his questions? Never have & never will.

* * *

geeze, look at me run on at the pen. will this please Goat? It sure as hell will tease Goat. but this is not what Goat gets to see, if he gets to see anything. i must remember this (a smile is just a smile, a kiss is just a kiss) & this is neither smile nor kiss—it's ink on paper & i can write anything i want because paper can be crumpled up & flushed or shredded & tossed ... this is not an indelible story.

who cares if it pleases him, it doesn't please me. it's taking on a life of its own, but it ain't my life. i swear on a stack of bibles. i don't know who this is. what product what package what price. but you Goat, you are my market. which makes this my promotion.

oh he could've been the champion copy writer of the world!

Does it tease you, Goat? It teases me, it does. like you teased me Goat, as you sat there, weary eyes looking into me ... i'd like to get to know you well ... like to get to know you, well. don't want to talk about the weather. don't want to talk about a girl named trudy ... don't want to hear the news 2day oh boy ... just like to get to know you well.

*   *   *

do you swing Goat? are you a wild thing Goat? wild thing. i think. i. fuck you.

let me take you for a ride. let me put the sparkle back into those weary eyes ... but you've got to trust me Goat, & trust the future, not linger on the past ... the unremembered past. Why would we want to put it down? why would we want to see what floats to the surface.

shit floats. & ivory soap. It floats.

*   *   *

What i liked about sitting in front of Goat was that i could see out his only window—good day sunshine: even though it was cloudy weather & rainy day people were walking by (walk on by, oh).

and for once, i'm an insider. i'm a sensation. you should've seen the sensation. 72 point headlines, & that was in the respectable newspapers.

but now i wonder, are my 15 andy worhal-whore-all promised minutes up? they must be up. i've tired of the wars, the kind of thing they sent me here for. i surrender all. all to him now i surrender. i surrender all.

am i allowed to give up & f-f-f-f-fade away?

* * *

no. this Goat seems to want something from me. the Truth. can't have it.

only a Goat would think it all right. (do you think it's all right to leave the kid with uncle ernie? yes i think it's all right. sure i think it's all-fucking-a-ok. right.)

so this bespectacled animal seems to think it's all right that i exercise my write in this my only visible means of communicating—but shall i be able to exorcise my wrongs?

* * *

& another dream I'm not telling you about, goat. yes, last night i had an even stranger dream. i dreamt that i was naked with a girl in front of god who blushed (god, not the girl) when i said, *but isn't this how it all began*? & he turned his back on me, & i relaxed into the darkness of his shadow.

* * *

well Goat, you said put it all down, even the dreams. & look at me go. you've got me cooking now. you're a persistent (and ugly) little fellow. you want the truth & nothing else—& you'll wait patiently for it to float up. not like the cops. the cops, what they want they take. if you fight back, they slap your face.

much simpler that, life with cops.

And goat is talking about writing again and i say to myself, as he talks about writing again, if you want me to write, i won't. & then he says, the bastard, he says if i don't write, that's okay too. & so i write, because i have nothing better to do than to steer this titanic endeavour through the ice floes to make sure i don't go down so that nothing floats up. sometimes nothing floats up; but often it does, so I don't want to go down, in case it comes up.

& then i figure it out—i figure out what it's all about—this is my ticket out. Goat is my ticket out. he's on my side. i've got to believe it. i've got to trust ...

gag ...

i know better than to trust.

*   *   *

go drown in it, fuck-face—in whatever comes up. go for a long walk off a short pier & see if you ever come up. or perhaps a fur ball will come up.

round ball round ball pull the bay's hair & cut it & cut it and tickle under there ...

but where is there?

that's what i put down. that's what came up. can i go now? there ain't anything buried in this davey jones locker of a soul. trust me.

*   *   *

here's one for you, Goat.

did you know moses was made of rubber?

it says in the bible that moses tied his ass to a tree & walked 40 miles into the desert. get it?

here's something coming up. in my life, i knew a few people who could get off on an ass like that ...

* * *

i told the moses joke during sunday school. i whispered it to a friend, at least i thought he was a friend. i mean he giggled at my joke & i laughed at his laughing. in fact, we laughed so hard i thought i was gonna pee my pants.

the teacher, Mr. B., came up to us & said: 'you've made the angels in heaven very unhappy by your actions 2day.' then he asked me what was so funny, he probably figured we were laughing at his acne or bald head. he said: 'confess, simon.' but i wouldn't.

so he asked my friend who was all ready turning red & starting to cry. why is it pricks like Mr. B. can pick out the weaker animals in the heard, cut them off, hog tie them & have their way with them?

(like me, eh Mr. B.)

so my friend confessed. he said: 'it's simon's fault. he told a dirty joke. i didn't mean to laugh. i'll ask for salvation. honest, Mr. B. i don't wanna go to hell. please don't tell my daddy.' That's what he said, the suck.

he even blurted out the joke between his tears & snivelling confession. & Mr. B. turned & slapped me once across the cheek, so hard that he knocked out a tooth & split my lip.

and i ran out of the classroom crying & bleeding, blood all over my crisp white shirt with the starched collar that always chafed my neck. i ran into the main auditorium, crying & bleeding, & disrupted the service until i found my daddy daddy daddy & i put my head in his lap for comfort.

& he asked me what happened & i told him the truth thru my tears & blood. i told him the truth because a little boy is supposed to tell his daddy daddy daddy the truth. i told him that the sunday school teacher had hit me & he asked me why & i said: because i told a joke. & my father, hearing my confession, slapped my other cheek.

but hey. i mean if you can't confess to our father which art on earth who else can you confess to, right? so i learned that confession was not good for the soul.

i mean he hit me across the other cheek, even harder than Mr. B. had hit me. right there in the middle of the church auditorium in the middle of the service. & his slap rang off the rafters. Talk about your turning the other cheek, or having it turned on you...

i was not a brave child, neither was i proud. i wept.

what are you crying about, my father said. if you don't stop crying now, i'll give you something to cry about.

and i stopped crying. just like that. & i swore i would never cry again. & i've kept my promise to myself, Goat, & you're not gonna break me just because you make me dive under the surface to see if shit floats!

and then an usher came along & smiled at my father who grunted at the usher & the usher ushered me out of the auditorium into a back room where ...

* * *

later that day, it was a spring day, after my mother applied ice packs to both sides of my face, after skipping sunday dinner, after sleeping off my pain, i went out into the back yard & sat on the back porch steps as the sun warmed me.

in the feeble garden my mother had begun to cultivate, i saw the earth move—a small mound heaved slightly. i plucked my hockey stick from out under the porch &, using the blade of my stick, i dug around the mound & unearthed a toad just coming out of hibernation. he blinked twice then closed his eyes as if to say, hey buddy can you spare me a few more winks.

i left him & went into the basement where i kept my supply of contraband firecrackers my friend's older brother had brought back from Buffalo for Victoria Day. i returned to the garden where the toad sat, eyes open now, celebrating spring: his rebirth.

he resisted not as i stuck a red cannon cracker into his mouth, lit the fuse, and... thy will be done thy kingdom come, on earth as it is ... as i blew that fucking frog to kingdom come ...

where is kingdom cum? any where near make-beleaf gardens?

* * *

we three kings from orient are/smoking here this rubber cigar/it was loaded & exploded/so here we are on yonder star ...

* * *

52

Write it all down & let it take you down ... to strawberry fields ... where nothing is real ... anywhere you want to go. Let it take you anywhere you don't want to go.

* * *

If it be thy will.

thy will be done. & i blew that frog to kingdom cum.

& ate his bloody remains.

* * *

my lawyer entered a plea of guilty by reason of insanity. the crown argued, half-heartedly. It was difficult to dispute his claim.

so here i am. Goat food.

* * *

christ you know it ain't easy. you know how hard-it-can be (ask any girl who slept with me, she'll tell you how hard-it-can be). the way things are going, they're gonna crucify me.

but not if Goat reads what comes up & likes it & proclaims the miracle cure. extra extra read all about it. pinball wizard in a miracle cure. extra!

* * *

the way things are going, the way these revelations are cumming, i'll soon be out: i AM A ViCTiM! my daddy slapped me when i went to him for comfort. so let me outta here already. (Oh this is cooking, i can feel freedom knock knock knocking on heaven's door.)

for fuck sakes, Goat, you're a wise man—you've got me (oh girl, you really got me) working in my medium. sure i'm rusty, blurry-eyed. but it's like getting on a bike after a long lay-off. hey, the crotch gets sore, but you get around, 'round, 'round… know what i mean?

look at me cycle. look at me float!

* * *

i'm so happy, i want to make the whole world laugh. so i'm gonna tell a joke. listen up:

jesus was wandering around heaven one day & came upon an old man resting on a cloud.

jesus said: hey old man, what are you up to. the old man said: i'm looking for my son. & jesus said: what a coincidence, i'm looking for my father. & the old man said: well, he's not really my son but he was like a son to me. & jesus said: gosh, the man i am looking for was not really my father but he was like a father to me. & the old man said: on earth, i was a carpenter & my son assisted me. & jesus said: on earth, my father was a carpenter & i assisted him. & the old man shook his head & said: as human as my son was, he was not quite human. like me, said jesus, i was not quite human.

& the old man & jesus embraced. Father, said jesus. & the old man smiled thru his tears & said: Pinocchio ...

* * *

i wrote the commercials that made the whole world buy.

imagine the possibilities ...

we mean business ...

every day, in every way, you're eating butter ...

there's no charge for the vrooom ...

hey toyota, you're pacific ...

molson golden. do you know what you're pissing ...

be the next one on your block to own a piece of the rock ...

why wait for winter. head south now ...

don't be a scrooge. this christmas, give blood ...

la la la la lada ...

eat shit. one million flies can't be wrong ...

we are the world. we are its chiclets ...

*   *   *

what came first, the chicken or the egg?

i did, the cock crowed.

*   *   *

did you hear the one about the agnostic, dyslexic insomniac? she sat up all night trying to prove the existence of dog. (arfarfarf)

*   *   *

this is almost too easy. i'm keeping my vow of silence, i'm committing no acts of violence & they must see i've gone clean (did you ever go clean?) & even though i haven't confessed that i'm the one who done the deed ('cause i didn't do the deed) (ph, good one) soon i shall so be freed. right? write!

i'll simply complete this project Goat has given me & present this, my head, to him, with two box tops from any cereal box, on a platter. what does it matter? i'll get a passing grade at this rate, & maybe time off for good behaviour

and then i'm outta here. on parole? Sure, but i'll stay clean: then they'll know i shouldn't've been here in the first place. outta my face. lost in space. the moon race. paper chase ... satin & lace. but can i keep up the pace ...

* * *

but what if they put lithium up my nose & i get hosed? but Goat is a very new age kind of guy. he wouldn't go for that truth serum, electro-shock, torture chamber kind of stuff. would ya, buddy?

he expects the truth & suspects the truth is what he'll get. so all i need to do is write this out—create a surface to delve beneath until i find a lump of coal. a lump of coal, you see, can be transformed under pressure and thru miracles into diamonds on the souls of my shoes. watch me sparkle. watch me shine.

& i had nothing to do with the shoeshine boy ... except i too was once a shoeshine boy. only i didn't make the news that day, oh boy. he left me alive. (who's he? how should i know; i don't have eyes in the back of my head.) & i told nobody. i even wiped clean the shoeshine wax from my ass. the wax he used to ride inside. so there is no evidence at all ...

there, how's that for floating up, Goat. how's that for true confession?

he rode me into hell, Goat. into hell ...

FOUR DAY FOUR DAY FOUR DAY FOUR DAY

There was an old man named Michael Finnegan.

He grew whiskers on his chin again.

The wind came out and blew them in again.

Poor old Michael Finnegan begin again ...

*   *   *

Yo, goat! last night i dreamt about shells. layers of shells. layers of star-shaped sea shells beneath which was hidden (can you believe it) identity. yep. hidden identity. shell game on a beach full of shells. & i had to identify identity. it was like trying to identify a lit match in hell.

i picked a shell & came up empty & owed the walrus running the show (i am the walrus, he said, koo-koo-ka choo) all that i had & all that i was & all that i ever could've been. in return for that i got nothing. lucky me. i think i won in losing. what the fuck would i do with an identity.

*   *   *

and last night, i went to football training camp in my dreams. a camp at which they trained us to kill. i had to demonstrate the emotion of a sheet of steel & i failed the test. metal fatigue, the coaches diagnosed as my problem because i melted down in tears & refuse to be a man.

* * *

i'm tired of dreaming. i want my blank night-mind back, Goat. give me liberty or give me Tv. Let Tv usher me back into my old fantasies, away from this ... (where does this come from?) ... this ... this usher who takes me from my father (who art in heaven, hollow by thy name) ... he drags me into a back room, sits me on a chair & says: i understand you've been a bad boy. do you know what happens to bad boys?

oh god, float away ...

you know what he did, Goat?

he pulled down my pants & turned me on his lap. yes, i knew what happened to bad boys. this was nothing new. this was simply a theme in variation. In classical music, how divine… in this? simply a variation on the theme, right daddy?, on what happens to bad boys bad boys whatcha gonna do bad boy…

* * *

So childhood, you elusive hood, you little red riding hood, you goldilocks mauled by the three bears, by the teddy bears picnic, by jack sprat would eat no fat, by jack be nimble jack be quick, by jack off ... so childhood. come out come out where ever you are.

* * *

Don't touch that dial. We'll be right back after this brief mess ...

* * *

Looking for something. don't know what it is ... can't get me outta my mind ... so i can get into who i am. but what if who i am is who i was ...

* * *

Round ball, round ball. Pull the baby's hair. & cut it & cut it & cut it & cut it & tickle under there.

But where is there?

* * *

Oh Goat, what am i doing here? why am i doing this? As i do this, all i see is a contented child raised on milk from contented cows. a child often alone but seldom lonely. a child who was a child who was a child. nothing more; nothing less. we were all children once. some of us are children still. so i grew up. what did you expect me to do? stay in the closet of childhood forever ...

i mean, there wasn't anything so extraordinary about it at all. it was. i was. & now here i am ...

so he kissed my ass. so?

& so he slid me off his lap, unZiPped his pants & asked me to kiss his ... and then to lollypop it, lollygag it... it was loaded & exploded ...

* * *

"Oh, like, okay,' i goes. 'Wow,' he goes. 'Like really?"

'Fer sure, like?'

'Oh like fer sure, yup. Fer sure.'

i heard them speak that way 2day, oh boy. & to think that they would soon be college grads. but i really impressed the student orderlies who were in the hall talking about whatever. i didn't cop much of a feel (there wasn't much there to cop, she was so skinny) but i got enough to see me thru 2nite ... & i think she's too embarrassed to complain. But not embarrassed enough to change her career ...

* * *

why is it, Goat, our conversations keep floating up. i thought i had put you out of my mind.

'There's no brutality here,' Goat said. 'only persuasion. mild persuasion, if you're open to it.'

But that's exactly how i approached them, Goat—with mild persuasion. & they were open to it. Only if persuasion didn't work, was i forced to use ...

who me? use brutality? never. trust me, I'd say. & they would.

* * *

i saw her picture in the paper. She collected Gumby & Pokey memorabilia. i went to see her show at the Gallery. i picked up her business card. the next day, i phoned & made an appointment to see her, one collector to another.

We met in the gallery one evening, after hours, to talk prices & share collector's experiences. There, amongst her plastic figures, i Gumbyed & Pokeyed her & Pokeyed & Gumbyed her.

The police released few details to the press other than to say that what had happened was bizarre. Yes it was. Almost as fucking bizarre as collecting Gumby & Pokey memorabilia.

There. A True confession. Ought to get you excited. Bet it's not in your files. it'd be in the police files under unsolved cases. so charge me. i'll plead insanity. & you'll have to keep me under for another two weeks.

that's if i'm telling you the Truth, goat. Could've picked up the story from a contact on the force be with you, you wouldn't believe what some of those a-holes on the force be with you are up to…

* * *

Lunch!

Baked beans (again). the food(!) has gone down, but i don't know if i can hold on to it. it's gonna come out one orifice or the other eventually—& maybe sooner than later.

What people do to let go of it all. Or is it they have nothing to hold on to? strange people i meet in bars, they tell me what they do to let go. i don't know why. i say nothing. i guess i just look as if i've never held on to anything in my life. so they think i'm safe to talk to. especially because i've perfected the perfect reply: the silent nod accompanied by the understanding smile.

One guy i met told me he went fishing every weekend. He never once caught a fish. He just sat there dangling his line in the water & got smashed. that's how he let go.

fun, eh. that was it. as far as i know, he's still fishing.

A lady i met in a library—i was reading Portnoy's Complaint & she struck up a whispered conversation— told me that she masturbated her cat. i have a face that people confess stuff like that to. So i mewed & she

61

laughed & took me home & made me watch her—1st she did the cat, then she did me ... then she had me do the cat, then do her ... then she spread Puss 'N Boots on her pussy and had the cat go down on her ...

& *then* it got bizarre.

A lady i met in a bar told me that every February, she went to Florida, to spring training, to screw baseball players. She was mostly into rookies, especially married rookies. Then all thru the season she'd ball baseball players. Once the world series was over, she'd go into sexual hibernation until spring training began again.

She's still doing it i suppose—all those nervous rookies getting their Louisville sluggers stroked.

i tell you their stories here to ask you this: who's crazy? Me? them? The fish? the cat? the ball players? who belongs in here?

under the circumstances, i have shown incredible restraint. i mean, the things that people do. & me, i just do my thing too.

*   *   *

do you want to know what my problem is, Goat? here's my problem:

When not in love, i eat. Not just like your average Canadian eats. When not in love, i eat food more like your average Zamboni eats ice shavings between periods at MakeBeleaf Gardens. Or your average bulldozer eats earth while tearing up trees for a new subdivision.

i eat like a high-price callperson satisfying a high-paying john's particular culinary fetish.

When not in love, i eat like a tornado demolishing a trailer park. i eat like a flock of seagulls cleaning up the aisle after a Jay's game at Exhibition Stadium. (think of all the starving seagulls since the Jays moved to SkyDome & started to play with the roof closed to keep mother nature out.)

When not in love, i eat dangerously, disregarding the maxim: 'For every action there is an equal & opposite reaction.' Which means, when not in love i eat & the world starves.

When starved for love, i eat... but am never satiated.

i was skinny when i lived with her, Goat. but then she started to get fat. i should've know it was baby fat. why'd she have to go do that? & so, i confess, i cut & ran. i ran home—to the empty house & set up house. there's no place like home, no place like home ...

& i ate & ate & ate. Lord, i did not miss a plate ...

*   *   *

Are you familiar, Goat, with the 3-day Labour Day Weekend novel-writing contest? A whole novel in three days. Can you dig it, Goat?

i know i'll never be one of the entrants, no. Never be. Hell, with writing as with love-making as with watching Tv (pick a show, any show, ZAP, too bad so sad, you missed it), i'm lucky if i last a minute, let alone three minutes, let alone three whole fucking days.

That's why i don't understand this Goat. i'm hard. i'm good & hard. i'm working good & hard. this is like prolonged sex. but where's the climax? the climax eludes me. it won't come any more ...

tell me i can stop Goat, it hurts to go on. tell me it is finished. Please. let it be. let it be finished ...

*   *   *

i used to be an advertising copy writer, you know. you've got my file. Wrote one-minute Tv commercials & that's how long i last in love. then came the channel changer—ZAP—& attention spans diminishes—ZAP—and i wrote thirty second commercials & that's how long i lasted—ZAP—in love—& then thirty-seconds was too long as attention spans diminished—ZAP—& somebody said: you got fifteen seconds.

& even that was too long for chronic ZAPpers.

& even that was too long for my love to last.

but long enough for 2 to threaten to become 3 ...

*   *   *

i used to be an advertising copy writer.

if you own something you do not need, something you never wanted, some fucking thing that amused you for a minute or thirty seconds or fifteen seconds or less, & now it takes up space in your garage, basement, closet or cupboard because you're too embarrassed to hold a garage sale to get rid of it ...

if you own something like a Pet Rock only dumber & larger or smaller, please forgive me. i am not laughing at you.

64

Most days.

*   *   *

hey Goat, here's a thought. what if this works. i mean. what if the operation is a success? this open heart lobotomy you're conducting with pen as scalpel.

what if i find my voice again? will i become a star? will you? will we appear on Gzowski, Carson, Donahue? or with fat black lady who became a skinny black lady who became fat black lady again. i read the tabloid headlines 2day, oh girl.

or if i find my voice will they crucify me, which is why they want me to speak, so they can nail the man they think i am to a cross & hang me out to dry.

you think i don't know how the system works.

they want somebody—anybody—to blame. they pluck me from the gutter & said: stand in line. they plucked another gutter dweller & said: look thru the mirror & identify him, number 666 as the man who did the deed, & we'll let you go on whatever charges we choose to fabricate against you.

do you think, if the oprah-ation is a suck-cess, i'll be a star? oh andy warhol andy whore-all, i can taste my 15 minutes ...

*   *   *

One o'clock. Two o'clock. Three o'clock. ZAP.

*   *   *

1967. Grade seven. Acne. Clearasil. B.O. Mandatory showers after gym. (Ve half vays to make you wet.) And i am falling in love, or in lust. (Stick with it. this could lead to full frontal nudity on the silver screen when they sell the movie rights. when i paint my masterpiece.) i am also failing history, which isn't the fault of any of the explorers we're studying. No. i'm falling & failing because of Peggy's garters.

You see, in history, i sit one row over & two seats back from Peggy. She wears mini-skirts that come up past the dark tops of her nylons (look ma, no panty hose) exposing the tips of her black garters.

i've only seen garters before in the skin books that my friends & i swipe from the Danny's variety store. (What's the statute of limitations on porn theft in this country?) In these books, women expose half-moon breasts, lace underwear &, my favourite, black garters thru transparent negligees. Dark rectangles cover their eyes & nipples.

On some pages, the women are kissed by men wearing t-shirts (wop shirts, we call them), neatly-creased trousers & polished shoes. The men don't have rectangles over their eyes.

Peggy doesn't wear rectangles over her eyes, either. i wish i could put rectangles over my eyes because, well, whenever i see Peggy's skirt creep above the horizon of the dark tops of her nylons exposing her garters, i have to place a text book in my lap to cover my, uh, you know what…

i'm failing history because i miss lectures, reading assignments & homework questions. i take lousy notes & i don't answer questions, not even when asked— because you are supposed to stand up to answer

questions, and I'd have to put the book in my lap down
... . Shit, all the guys know why i have a book in my lap.
some of the girls know too. Peggy knows, the way she
smiles just so. So i won't stand up to answer their
questions. & because of her garters, i'm failing history,
as she wriggles in her seat, exposing even more garter
& thigh & i wriggle in my seat, exposing even more
ignorance on the subject that i am doomed to repeat.

* * *

hey, look what just floated up. two lines from the first
poem i ever wrote: The Tree

The tree was a symbol of the world—

For it was a knotty tree.'

(Arrrrrrrrrrgh. how come i can't flush such impotent stuff
from my mind, Goat, yet the important stuff remains
lodged in some obscure corner of some obscure closet
...) (You think i don't know?)

imagine such a Truth as The Tree now decomposing in
an overflowing landfill ... the pencil lead & paper bleach
contaminating some precious water supply. imagine the
worms slithering thru its serious intent as they chew it up
& defecate. a well-deserved fate, i'd say. but then, who
am i?

am i like my tree—Knotty?

* * *

Food. they call this food? i'm not in love. i need a big
meal deal where 2 can dine for 4.99 (it's my line!)

Well, watch me eat it anyway, like a flock of vultures celebrating another rank carcass ripe for the picking. & you may begin to understand how not in love i am.

* * *

'Baby & me was ripe for the picking. That was the day we ran into Albert Flasher.'

if you know what that song was about, please let me know. Then there'll be two of us who know.

* * *

i never sent away for the glasses that were advertised in the back of the comic books i swiped as a kid—the magic glasses that promised x-ray vision. The ads always showed a guy wearing the glasses & looking through a wall at a busty lady. What he saw was this: the outline of the woman thru her clothes.

There were always question marks over the woman's head, as if she were wondering who had stripped her without her feeling a thing & there were always exclamation marks over the voyeur's head, as if were wondering how he ever got so lucky.

Of course, i always wanted to know what was beneath the clothes of ladies. But i never sent away for the glasses.

see. i wasn't all bad.

Of course, i might've sent money for the glasses if it weren't for the 99¢ (U. S.) plus postage & handling i had already wasted on the Ventriloquists Helper (a small metal button you held against the inside of your lips with your tongue). it was supposed to let me throw my voice.

'Amaze & your friends!' 'Startle your dog!' 'Make plants & rocks & other objects speak!' 'Project rude noise from strange places!'

in the illustration advertising the ventriloquists helper, there were always question marks over the heads of guys who where watching a rock speak or over the head of the confused dog who was listening to a fire hydrant berate him or over the head of an embarrassed girl who was covering her backside as a group of giggling guys listen to rude noises emanating from her rear.

Always, lurking around some corner lapping up the confusion & chaos he was creating lurked the ventriloquist who was throwing his voice with the help of the Ventriloquist's Helper.

& of course over his head, a dove. & as he threw his voice to the sky & thundered: 'this is my beloved son in whom i am well pleased.' daddy was never well pleased with me. he was never ever pleased.

All i ever got from the Ventriloquist's Helper was a mouthful of rusty-tasting saliva & a painful chancre on the tip of my tongue. As for my voice, i never did throw it, but i sure as hell managed to lose it.

That's why i didn't spend any money on the x-ray glasses. i was afraid of what i wouldn't see because i figured the glasses wouldn't work. Or was it that i was afraid of what i would see if they did—might i look at myself in the mirror & see thru me ...

* * *

Goat, am i trying too hard to please you?

* * *

this should've been the first thing i wrote whenever it was i began to write:

Beware. Start with this. i am not me. i am a liar. Or an actor, but not out on loan. & definitely not a dog without a bone. Arf! Arf! This is Tv. 32 lines per second coming at you. i am not you; you are not me. Who's watching who here? i am the Walrus. You are the polar bear. Let's go see. You are solid. You are chocolate. You are the Easter Bunny. i am the tooth. Fairy.

& before you begin (Even though you've already begun) read my disclaimer: *i used to be a fucking advertising copywriter.* like the disclaimer i put at the beginning of my most famous commercial: a five-minute job that ran during the National News. i put it there, my disclaimer, to prevent you from ZAPping. 'Sex & violence. Full frontal nudity.' it worked. the ratings for my masterpiece came in higher than ratings for the Grey Cup or Stanley Cup or Stupor Bowel. Not a soul dared ZAP out. i am a genius. Ask my ex-boss. Ask the raise in my pay. i could've been the champion copywriter of the world.

instead, i woke up got outta bed dragged a comb across my head ... saw my father on his death bed ... saws myself with x-ray eyes ... knew i was my old man in disguise ... and lost my voice.

What happened that night i ran home, Goat? what has been happening ever since?

There's something there. It's why i'm here.

* * *

1965. Warp-time. i am in grade five. i put a dot of ink on the knuckle of my right index finger. (Pay attention now or ZAP outta here.) i make the OK sign with my left thumb & left index finger (had i done it with my left foot, i would've won an Oscar). i bent my right index finger & slipped the OK sign tightly over my knuckle. Then i stuck my hands in front of Christine, the only girl with breasts in grade five, and said:

The aliens have landed. Have no fear. This one's friendly. if you kiss him, he'll bring you good luck.

a confession. i didn't really know what i was doing. you see, most guys were just as naive as most girls. it's just that we were vulgar shits. Nor did Christine know what she was doing as she giggled & bent & kissed my alien. & the guys watching bust a gut laughing & the girls watching muttered: Tsk. Tsk. Ooo-yuk. Oh gross. Christine did not know (how could she know) that i was lying. The alien was not friendly. Like me, he was a prick.

* * *

Yes, as a child, i had a Tv for a baby sitter. i watched shows from start to finish. (i actually *had* an attention span.) Every image held my attention. Even commercials. Somewhere, somehow, something happened. A wire came loose. You begin to short-out. Then you short-circuit. But the images kept on coming— faster faster faster faster ... & then they got s o s l o w a n d p r e d i c t a b l e ... & you had to search the tube over and over and over for images worth watching.

You start your search with serious intent around the time you sprout your first pubic hair. On some shows, the women wore less clothes than on others—those were images worth watching. Around the time that you develop acne, women began to take off their clothes on Tv—sometimes against their will, which was even more worthwhile.

Then things get even better (for better or for worse) with the arrival of CiTY Tv & the Baby Blue movie—women take off all their clothes, at will, against will, with Will, with Wilma, with or without Willy. Willy-nilly. so then the competition follows suit. at least as far as people stepping outta their suits & skirts & blouses & shirts.

'Sex sells,' the station master(baters) proclaimed. & soon women take off their clothes all around the dial, day or night, especially on CBC (english and french channels) & TvO (the pubic channels). in fact, events move so fast, especially after midnight, that you have to sit real close to the Tv & turn that dial to find the best spot for a hot shot—explicit images to curl your short & curlies even curlier. Oh brave nude world.

& soon progress marches on and more and more channels can be found on the dial & ZAP! ... the remote control channel changer is born ... oh braver newer nuder world! & Tv watching has over 30 flavours to choose from—& i eat them all up, oh smorgasbord delite!

if Freud were alive (the Freuds are alive, with the sound of ZAPping) he'd say that marketers fulfil the dreams of the modern age. if you're thirsty but wary of tap water, they serve you bottled water. if you're in a hungry & in a hurry & not nutritious conscious, they serve you anything you want as fast as you want it. if you're lazy, suffering from inertia & don't want to get off the couch to change the channel—ZAP—the genies pop out of their bottle to fulfil your wish & they serve you the remote channel ZAPper.

*　　*　　*

i got a brand pair of roller skates, you've got a brand new key ... i got a brand new colour Tv, you've got a brand new ZAPper. i think that we should get together & live happily ever after ...

*　　*　　*

So i got me a channel ZAPper & began ZAPping from 32-line image to 32-line image. Could heaven offer anything better than this? Oh boy what joy & bliss. i'm gonna sit on couches of gold. i'm gonna watch & never get old. is heaven better than this? Oh boy. What joy & bliss.

*　　*　　*

Karma Sutra newest position: whatever position you're in—when the view gets boring, change the scene without changing your position. in comparison, the Joy of Sex was manual labour—something you had to work at: & as we all know, work is no fun: oh modern age: oh modern cage: oh modern couch spud all the rage.

so why the rage? but why no outrage?

And soon there were even more naked images (women only, of course, except for the occasional male buttocks) from which to choose in a multi-lingual selection.

Let it rain on me. For i have found nirvana on Tv—
heaven on earth: me & my ZAPper & a little slip of the
zipper.

* * *

don't touch that dial.

excuse me, but fuck you.

Don't throw out the baby with the bath water.

excuse me, but ... but? but what? who? tickle under
where?
ZAPZAPZAPZAPZAPZAPZAPZAPZAPZAPZAPZAPZA
PZAPZAPZAPZAPZAPZAP

Don't throw out the past with the future. Don't throw out
the future with the present. Save water. Shower with a
friend.

ZAPping lets you know that there is nothing you have to
do. There may be things you could do or want to do, but
there is nothing you have to do. The church, the state,
the family, your peers… they all make you feel you that
there are things you have to do. But there is nothing…

so let me outta here. i won't do nothing, i promise i
promise.

* * *

hey, i feel like crying, Goat. i must be getting better. this
writing is working. i feel like crying, which is weird.
because i don't do this sort of thing. Men don't. it's like
eating quiche. But i eat quiche. Does that mean that I am
not a man? Am i what I see in the screen… perhaps
nothing but the dot that fades away after the late late late

show ends & the Tv is turned off... why don't you all f-f-f-f-fade away...

But soft, what light thru yonder window breaks? it is VCRs & cable-TV with 24-hour movie, news & music video channels. it is hope for happiness eternal ...

*   *   *

Where have all the existentialists gone? long time passing ... Where have all the flower children gone? following the Grateful Dead ... Where have all the discos gone? still sucking ... Where has Paul McCartney gone? shit, he's still singing ...

*   *   *

in an old cedar chest in the basement of my deserted house that i ran back to when i ran away from her, i found Superman comic books, a Crown Royal bag full of marbles, a bag of green plastic toy soldiers, several Jell-O hockey coins, my collection of American pennies, a Salada tea box full of little ceramic bird figures, my grade one perfect-attendance medal (1st & last i ever received), a sea shell (from where?), a faded package of ladyfinger firecrackers, Jell-O car coins, a complete set of 1961 Toronto Make Beleaf hockey cards, a penny flattened by a train when i left it on a rail road track, a rusty peace symbol ... & a B&W photograph ... the kid in the picture looks like me, but the lady ... looks like nobody i've ever met before ...

*   *   *

Blind. i peer into darkness & find you hiding from memory. it must be tag you're it, home-sticker. Come out. Come out wherever you are.

Blind. i must be blind man's bluff. Pin the tail on the donkey. Spin me around until i'm dizzy, dizzy. Hush-a. Hush-a. round ball round ball cut the baby's hair ... we all fall down around the mulberry bush, the mulberry bush, the mulberry bush. Here we go round the mulberry bush ... A little doggie picked it up & put it in his pocket ...

& tickle & tickle & tickle & tickle & tickle ... under there ... but where is there? it doesn't tickle ... it hurts ... it hurts. it doesn't tickle under there ...

and where am i under now? it's dark, so dark. & smells of old socks. shoes. dark ... & shoes on the floor. closet. hall closet. when i hide there he can't tickle me until it hurts ... he who? & how long do i hide in the dark? how long has this been going on? how long do i hide from the hurt?

*   *   *

Goat, where did all the blackness come from? Blown in by the wind; I don't want to begin again ... I don't want to be ... in the basement where i grew up. when i cut her & ran home & hid in the basement where i grew up, the cellar where i threw up ... & i discovered the dark ... oh Goat, i discovered the dark ... i discovered hell in the dark ...

5th DAY

Wake up little suzy, you've got to go home.

           *   *   *

what was all that shit yesterday? a dream a dream. that's all it was, Goat. just a dream.

if so, how did it get into the end of yesterday's journal and not into the beginning of 2day's? Good question, Goat. you're a wise one you are. yes you are my little billy Goat, but don't be so gruff. it was friction, Goat— where fact grates up against fantasy ... it wasn't me ... it was copy writing; it was somebody i read about in the newspapers; it was movie-of-the-week on Tv; it was tabloid sleaze-oid ...

           *   *   *

ah, but now that I'm here, let me wipe the remaining sleep from my eyes & jot down the dream i do remember.

i was sitting at the kitchen table playing one of those kid's iQ tests—you know the one, where you're given a plastic hammer & different shaped pegs & have to hammer the square-shaped peg into the square hole & the star-shaped peg into the star hole & the ass-shaped peg into the ass hole ...

i have a hammer & i have a square peg & i hammer like an angry carpenter, trying to ram the square peg into the round hole. after a great amount of pounding, i succeed:

the hole is completely bent outta shape & the peg is totally twisted. but it fits ...

*   *   *

if i had a hammer, i'd hammer in the morning. but if i were a carpenter, would you marry me any way? would you be my lady? joseph was a carpenter; my father was a carpenter ... am i a square peg? what is the round hole i've been forced into? do i fit? is this success?

oh Goat, does this have you salivating, my self-analysis? does this have you masturbating, my dream-analysis? does this have you fornicating, your psycho-analysis? Careful, Goat—i'll report you to the authorities: Psychiatrist masturbates over patient's analysis of dreams. you'll be disbarred or de-frocked or whatever they do to Docs ...

*   *   *

so then why is it, if i'm a square peg, that i'm afraid of needles. i don't know why. it's not all that unusual, having fears or phobias. the woman i lived with (never mind the weather, tell me how is trudy?) she feared snakes—if only she had known that she was living with one! her archetypal nightmare cum true.

Actually, it's not so much needles i fear as it is self-professed sharp-witted people who reveal how dull & dumb they are.

*   *   *

She was not supposed to get pregnant. We had an agreement. she wanted me so badly that she didn't ask why i made her agree to it. she just figured i didn't wanna have kids. But she broke our agreement, Goat. she broke it & i broke her.

Then i broke away.

                    *   *   *

Richard's in on a break-a-way. He shoots. Bower, a sensational save!

did YOU see that, daddy? Bower a sensational save.

Yeah, simon. shut-up and watch the game.

saturday night. Hockey Night in Canada night. the make-beleafs vs. les canadiens ... saturday night. bath night so I'd be scrubbed clean for Sunday school... everybody ought to go to Sunday school, Sunday school, Sunday school. Everybody ought to... if i co-operated, i got to stay up & watch the whole game.

be a good boy, simon. do as i say. take your bath & get into your pyjamas and you can watch the whole game.

even the 3-star selection, daddy?

just be a good boy and do as i say ...

but what was it that he said?

                    *   *   *

At 33, after a life of saving, chastising & healing, Christ was crowned King of the Jews & crucified ...

At 33, after a life of battling, conquering & ruling, Alexander the Great, his place secured history, died ...

At 33, after a life of making people laugh, or not so much in my case, John Belushi, died of an overdose of cocaine and heroin... Oh, and at 33, after a life of fuck herr hitler, Eva Braun, committed suicide is painless... At 33, after a life of, singing the blues, or was it soul music? I dunno, singing whatever he sang, Sam Cooke was murdered... Was that the day the music died? I never did understand that song... but speaking of American Pie, Theo Van Gogh, the Dutch art dealer and brother of the ear cutting painter, duck his dick in one last disgusting well and died, at 33, of syphilis... Wonder if he was fucking, through some feat of time travel, Althea Flynt, the pornographer's wife, who drowned due to heroin overdose at, you guessed it, 33. Just like don't cry for me Argentinean Eva Peron... don't cry for me Goat because, at 33, after a life of eating cheese-flavoured popcorn, drinking the official beer of the Whatever Olympics, & ZAPping endless channels by remote control, i declared myself a brain-dead couch potato & tried to f-f-fade away ...

*   *   *

To think, they thought me brilliant. i have the awards to prove it. To think, i believed the proof. as if it were in the pudding. Stuck in my thumb, pulled on my plumb & fucked everybody in the agency without concern for race, creed, religion or sexual orientation.

But that was a short season. such a sweet bloom for such a short season. Then back to my real vocation— hiding in the basement.

*   *   *

Hey, look. i could be an alcoholic or a drug addict but i am neither. (although i am sometimes either.) i am brave. When i put on my brave face, or when i shave or go unshaven, i face life sober. Understanding my potential, i refuse to plunge into the depths of despair. i refuse to shop the drug-store of life, refuse to dull the pain of dullness. i recognize the only escape from this nonsensical existence, but refuse to take the detour to get me there any quicker than i am (we are) going going gone ...

*   *   *

Do i sound depressed? Ha! it's worse than that. i am depressing.

*   *   *

i could be a sex maniac (which has nothing to do with sex & everything to do with maniac). in fact you probably think i am. Let me tell you, it's not worth the effort. You should be glad i think this way. You should wish everybody did.

*   *   *

One of the inmates in here (one of the folks who actually belongs in here) walked past my door & said this to one of his (prime)mates: 'GERALD GOT HiS PHONE CALL FROM GOD.'

well, gol-ly.

So there I sat and that line defied me: do something with me, if you dare.

imagine what a writer would do with such a line. it begs me though to play the role created just for me that of God. & to call this thing called Gerald... & say what? Exactly ... A writer could do something with that line. but a copywriter? So i relinquish copyright. Take my words, please.

81

*   *   *

i'm tired. i'm so tired. breakfast has barely been served. i've just got here. Goat is watching, as he does, as I write. Occasionally he says, 'so?' as if there is something to so about or so something I am supposed to do with it... he chitter chatters. Or sits there stone cold silent, but yet content. Either way, I write. Occasionally I grunt... spout a few words... I dunno where this is supposed to go or how it will get me out of here. I have to finger that out, but... i'm tired. i'm so tired, and shit, goat, I've got a full day before me yet ... & yet?

to think what i might have been.

to think what once had been ...

*   *   *

in the museum program publicizing an exhibit of fossils that once had been my childhood, there is a black & white photograph of me—the only one remaining from the 4-for-a-quarter pictures i took in the curtained booth at the shopping mall the first time i swiped money from my mother's purse.

this child, the archaeologist's write-up accompanying the photograph asserts, was alive during the Plasticine period (although it is doubtful anybody noticed) & he is presumed to have died shortly after completing the finger-paintings his mother refused to tape to the fridge. several insignificant fragments were preserved amongst the dust balls that accumulated under the bed he wet almost every night. the exhibit also includes my report cards complete with D's, E's & F's & teacher's comments: refuses to participate - contributes nothing to class - is listless & bored - disrupts others - picks his nose - smells of urine - enjoys finger-painting

& visitors may listen to time-warped tapes of old friends chanting: stepped on a crack, you broke your mother's back - fatso is stupid fatso is stupid - liar liar pants on fire, got hung up on the telephone wires - you looked you looked you dirty crook you stole your mother's pocket book

(how did they know?)

the brochure also describes how my skull was found buried in the playground sand pit where i hid to escaped schoolmates bragging about gold stars & straight A's ...

petrified, he stuck it out in his new habitat until his fossilized remains were exhumed for exhibit in this hermetically-sealed display case illuminated by ...

... life flashes before my eyes ... but it is not my life! whose life is it, any how?

only they do not see how kaleidoscopic the finger-paintings were: as unsettled as fine sand sifting thru the sieve of time.

*   *   *

Goat, give me one, one & only one, good reason why we're here (because we're here because we're here because we're here).

Convince me that it's worth it. Convince them. Convince yourself. Go on. i'll count to three ...

ZAP.

*   *   *

AiDS?

Like a true nature's child, we are born, born to die.

ted's dead. now you know how he died.

What's that buzz, tell me what's a-happening.

it happened to ted & it can happen to you.

*   *   *

Graffiti in a Kingston, Ont. restaurant:

BORN NiCE

Ain't no bikers eating here, 'cept for the mountain biker variety. Yahoo! Mountain Dew.

*   *   *

You always hate the one you don't love. You always hate the person before you kill it. That makes it unworthy of anything but extinction. Like so many gooks.

*   *   *

No, i don't remember where i was the day that JFK was assassinated. Furthermore, i don't give a fuck where you were either.

*   *   *

Loneliness is a Tv set tuned to Jeopardy when your partner bursts into the room all excited about something & you shush her & only later realize, after you've incorrectly answered Fast Foods for $200 Alex, that you don't have anybody to talk to.

i'm sorry ted.

*   *   *

Fear is having nobody around, especially when you're wondering who made the sound you hope you didn't hear but know you did.

Like when i went back to the past, to the house, my house—the house where i grew up, threw up ...
 Squatting in the house: i heard a noise and hid in the closet, in the dark musty closet where i even found a pair of my old man's slippers & sucked on them for old time sake ... i heard a noise—or did i? is it just my imagination running away with me?

it sounds like fee-fi-fo-fum, i smell the blood of ...

the giant coming for me again.

the noise was my past erupting like a volcano ... hot and liquid in my face ...

i should've stayed there the first time until i rotted. i stayed there the second time until i rotted, didn't i? or at least until i got rotten ... yep, i just had to come out again, didn't eye? But who did i come out as? & Why?

*   *   *

it's why i'm here isn't it Goat? Because i came out of the closet again ...

is that what this is supposed to be about? My second coming out?

*   *   *

i felt as confident as the iceberg that had TitANiC labelled on its underbelly as i headed towards him. You're going down tonight, asshole, going down ... ZAP ... London Bridges going down going down going down ... ZAP ... Lloyd Bridges going down, going down ...

85

*   *   *

jesus was cross. He got really hammered. He said, 'Spill the wine, take this girl. Spill the wine.' Nah. He said, 'You're the boss. Forgive those suckers.' This he said when others would've only stammered yammered blubbered babbled. Tower of babel. Tower of Love. Love potion number nine. Revolution number nine. Number nine. Number nine. Ninety-nien Red Balloons ...

if ted had used a red balloon he might still be alive. The prick. And trudy too. She would've never met me, not like that, if ted were still alive, the mutherfucking cheating prick.

*   *   *

jesus was cross but up there he showed his intestinal fortitude. The guard with the spear made sure of that.

Oh, there is power power wonder working power in the blood (in the blood) of the lamb (of the lamb ... BAH BAH black sheep have you any wool ...)

*   *   *

Her breasts could've been packed in a crate & shipped from California (dreamin' on such a summer's day) to Toronto—so compact & firm they were ...

& i've seen longer legs, legs i thought would never end, but only on a giraffe ...

*   *   *

Goat, this is all so ... All so what? i've confessed to nothing. i will confess to nothing. You give me pen you give me paper. You give me the tools to forge my own confession. But you don't understand, forgery is all i am capable of. i've learned long ago how to put down lies. After all, I am a copywriter. so how can you trust me? are these not just more lies? can you believe the lies i put down even as they float above the surface. With nothing to implicate me. i know nothing more than any man could've heard on the news 2day, oh boy. the english army had just won the war.

*   *   *

all ready the lies begin. these words are too hard, too heavy, to float up anywhere. 2morrow, what am i to do with this? to start, that was my first mistake.

no, to be born. that was my first mistake. but then i had no choice. i wasn't born this way. & now?

They got the wrong man, Goat, because they ain't got every man. Trust me on that. i am no Christ. i will not bear the burdens of the world. and if you insist that this is how i shall pass my time, then so be it. But i must warn you, i will simply scribble across the page nonsensical ink blots signifying nothing. Sure, subject to your interpretation. Go ahead. You'll not be the first to misinterpret me. Go ahead. Give me your psychological head, Goat. Head cheese, Goat. Give it me. Give me your best. i'll do my best to give you my worst.

And then if you wish, you can complete the false frame that imprisons me here & now.

*   *   *

So, shall i start at the beginning for you, even though we are part way thru?

*   *   *

i don't know if watching Tv, looking thru my fantasy window, kept me out of trouble as a child, out of danger as an adolescent, out of touch as an adult. i don't know.

What would i have done without it? Bugged my parents more? Become a juvenile delinquent? Necked with girls? Changed my world? Changed the world?

i doubt it. Doubt it doubt it.

But what would they have done without me??? Oh Captain Kangaroo(court). Rin Tin Tin. Lassie. Sky King. The Lone Ranger. Cisco Pike. The Real McCoys (Well, there's grandpapy Amos & the girls & the boys & they're known as the family called the real McCoy's). Danny Thomas. Leave it to Beaver (cleaver—the beaver cleaver). Huckle Berry Hound Dog. Bugs & the gang, especially Daffy Duck. Mickey Mouse (Donald Duck). (Forever let us hold our banner high high high.) (i get high with a little help from my friends.) (Do you need anybody? i need something to watch.) Friendly Giant. Magilla Gorilla. The Flintstones (meet the Flintstones they're a modern stone-age family). Rocky & Bullwinkle. Commander Tom. i love Lucy (how i loves ya, how i loves ya, Lucy). (You picked a fine time to leave me Lucille.) Red Skeleton. Ed Sullivan. Batman. Superman. Everybody on Gilligan's island (ya got to believe there was stuff goin' on on that island that we never got to see…. The Beverly Hillbillies (come listen to my story about a man named jed, poor mountaineer barely kept his family fed, & then one day he was shooting at some food & up thru the ground came a bubbling crude ... oil that is, black gold. tex-ass tea. well the 1st thing you know old jed's a millionaire, the kin folks say jed, move away from here. they say California is where you ought to be, so they loaded up there truck & moved to beverly—hills, that is. swimming pools, movies stars, cement ponds ... Petticoat Junction (at the junction petticoat junction). Green Acres. Hogan's Heroes. Rat Patrol. The Flying Nun. Dick Van Dyke. My Mother the Car. All in the Family. Our pet Juliet. Hockey Night in Canada (hello Canada ... live from make-beleaf gardens). Star Trek—space, the final frontier... that's what Tv was to me, it was my space, my place—my final frontier ...

And of course, all our wonderful sponsors. (Thank you for inviting us into your homes.) & i watched faithfully— for what is life without commitment & loyalty—excluding the cancelled shows ...

*　　*　　*

i cannot help it. i'm a man, even if i am not much of one. i'm as vain as a peacock, as cowardly as a hyena, as ugly as a duck-billed platypus, as cocky as a rooster, as stubborn as a jackass, as dumb as an ox (which is to insult to oxen of the world). As vicious as ... a man. i am. We are.

Help. We need somebody. Not just anybody. We need somebody to hate.

*　　*　　*

may i wax philosophical, Goat? allow me this because you got me thinking, Goat (i must be getting desperate or really bored if i've resorted to thinking).

but this is it, one of those eureka moments. i figured out what this is all about, what you're after Goat. the key to my freedom is in sight. try this on:

maybe my silence is the problem. you see, maybe the problem is my silence. maybe the problem is every man's silence. maybe the problem is that men don't talk. that men don't talk to other men, never mind that they don't talk to women or dogs, or Goats, or whomever. maybe the problem is that men don't talk at all. even to themselves.

or if they do talk, they mutter and don't listen. if somebody else—another man, woman, child—tries to talk to them, men don't listen. i mean, if you knew that you wanted to seduce your daughter, for instance, or fuck the shoeshine boy, who would you talk to? whomever you talked to would put you away or have you put away. so you don't talk.

so maybe that's why men do what they do. they don't talk, they just do. since they cannot confess they repress until they explode. & all they are left with, if they're left with is the ability to deny if they can find a voice, or remain silent on the grounds that anything else may discriminate against me because I'm a man, yes I am I'm a man…

i mean, look at the shape of the world. imagine if the men said, hey, we're really fucking things up aren't we? but we can't talk about it. except for a few empty platitudes, some disguised as religion & some as philosophy, we're sworn to silence, like our fathers & our fathers' fathers ad nauseam … they'd put us all away if we confessed or admitted or or or… we're like … like vampires. waiting for the silver bullet (hi-ho, silver) or the stake.

right? Write? Left-right...

*   *   *

(is that the answer, Goat? am i cured? can i go home now?)

*   *   *

no? try this then: maybe if men were allowed to be human, they would act more humane. that's not an excuse, nor is it a rationalization. it's by no means a justification either. it's barely a theory or a premise or a supposition. it might qualify as an empirical deduction. all geese are white, i thought, until i saw a black goose. All geese arc gccse, I thought, until I saw a mongoose...

hell, it's hardly more than words on a page, scrambled like the pieces of a jig-saw puzzle i can't put together.

you put the puzzle together, Goat. tell me what you want me to see so i can see it for you & get the fuck outta here.

...you know what you're gonna find if you put the puzzle together? you'll find a very dark & secret place where men go, even though they're terrified of the dark. it's to the dark they go to hide themselves & hide from themselves. but sometimes, men step out into what they perceive of as light & then ...

but what am i telling you this for. you're a man. you can't hear me. which is why it's no use talking to you.

but why am i here, Goat. i hid in the darkness as best as i could. i hid in the darkness until it bled daylight. is that why i'm here? i stepped out into the light?

i don't remember. i honestly don't. remember.

*   *   *

ah, but if men could dance naked in the sunshine, be cleansed by the light, & not be ashamed ... that would be healthy, that would be good ... if only men could talk themselves into the light. if only men could talk.

But i'm not certain that this is at all so, you see, i cannot verify it. in fact, i didn't even write it. i sure as hell didn't say it & i doubt that i even thought it. actually, i read it in a magazine i snuck out of the Tv room when man-mountain went to take another shit.

oh what has become of me? writing journals, reading magazines & not watching Tv.

and even if i did talk, there are no men with whom i could talk to, talk about it, whatever it is. & even if there were, they would not listen. & even if they heard me, against their will, they would deny it. What ever it is i have or have not said.

So i confess. I am a man. I must be guilty.

Crucify me. crucify me.

*   *   *

the way things are going, they're gonna crucify me.

*   *   *

Yummy yummy yummy i got love in my tummy & it's distorted by acid indigestion.

*   *   *

1964 floats up. i'm 8 years old, in grade 4. it's track-and-field day. (Do you guys who were fat-ass chubbies once remember track & field day? Of course you do. Memories like that we can't repress, no matter how hard we try.)

i wanted to stay home—i had a cold & a sore knee, but really i had a need to not be left out in the cold—to not be embarrassed on the field. but mother wouldn't let me stay home. because that would embarrass her.

i don't fucking believe it. They're insisting that i run the 100-yard dash. Why can't they leave me alone? Who told them i was hiding behind the portable? Rat Fink. You, you dirty rat ...

Get yer paws off me, assholes, is what i'd like to have had the courage to say as they shoved me to the starting line where a bunch of guys wearing PF Flyers, shorts & t-shirts are at their mark. i'm wearing a long-sleeved shirt, corduroy trousers (chubbies) & imitation Hush Puppies bought at Eaton's Bargain Basement.

The grinning, asshole principal, with acne scars that pot-mark his face, says, Ready-Set-Go. & we're off. Well, everybody else is off. i am moving but it's more like a Jell-O waddle. & all the jerks on the sidelines are hooting. Even Pimple-face is laughing.

So i stop in the middle of the race (all the others have crossed the finish line ages ago anyway) & i say to the Pimple what, up until now, i have only said behind his back: 'When you were a teenager did you play goalie for your high school dart team?'

He's a bug. My mouth is Raid. Kills laughter dead on contact.

but in the office, Zit-Head gives me fifty lashes across each hand. i don't cry. i don't even whimper. i have discovered something stronger than violence. He can beat the fuck outta me & it doesn't matter. He's lost it. i have discovered the power of absolute disrespect.

As much as he hates me, he knows i hate him that much more. but that doesn't stop him from demonstrating the extent of his hate, as he makes me drop my drawers & gives me fifty lashes more ...

*   *   *

Goat, who thought this shit up? i mean shit floats, right, but ... it's not worth the effort. it's not worth the effort. it's not. not. not.

*   *   *

Last night, what floats in from down the hall ... TV sounds that i ignore. and thee girls on the couch, Lard-asses Harem. They're at it again:

Goat, why don't you put them on this regimen? then you'd really see shit float!

*   *   *

Goat, if i were brilliant like they said i was, if i were the writer you said i was, i would have done something with this: my sci-fi novel: *The Hyper-Tech Picasso ii Dream-Weaver State of Being*. i would have at least written more than the title.

*   *   *

That's one small step for (static). One large step for (there's no static cling) ...

*   *   *

Ah, you let me go... at least out or your office, and what have I done since? I haven't the foggiest... how these drugs make me foggy....

my how the light grows dim. i didn't eat my dinner yet. or my lunch come to think on it. & is this my breakfast tray i see before me? it grows dim, it grows dim, i shall lift my skirt & expose a shin... but wait, what soft light thru yonder window breaks... it is the a.m., which explains the breakfast tray...

SIXTH DAY, THE

White walls surround me. This could be a mental health centre, but it's not. it must be home—what's that familiar buzz, tell me what's a-happening, i hear down the hall? the three stooges, still crazy after all these years, on the late late show. lard-ass & his harem must be getting extra Tv time for goo-goo behaviour. piss on 'em. That is what I shall do when I gain my revenge for this, or that, or this and that. For what they do and don't let me do due overdue to do it to them. Piss on 'em...

*   *   *

So, I have some time before we meet again, my friend... and a cut to mend from when I tried to piss on them, all before we meet again, some day soon, we shall meet again... we shall overcome, my sweet lord, one day...

*   *   *

The eyes are the first to go. They stumble like a prisoner, confined to a cave of darkness since birth, liberated by those with good intentions. Blinded by the light, even that of night. But worse by day. Hey hey. Hey hey.

*   *   *

Driverless auto careens thru decades. Rusted out, burnt out '54 Chevy hits scrap heap without impact ...

is that what i fear? A collision with destiny without impact? Does that fear keep me immobilized here? Should that fear not inspire me to rush headlong,

96

headstrong, hard-headed hard-on into whatever? Or is it failure that i fear? if i were to make the effort & still made no impact ... is that the failure that i fear?

i have nothing to fear but fear itself, and fearless platitudes ...

*   *   *

Well hello, goat. I still this is weird, me here, you there, pen and paper here, and tickle under there... i still remember it as if it were my last birthday. Perhaps that's because it happened on my last birthday. Or at least on the last birthday i remember.

i came home drunk drunk drunk at 3 am. My how the light had grown dim. & passed passed passed out on a couch in front of the Tv set which i forgot to turn off when i went out, which was still waiting for me like a faithful pet ...

& i passed out but came to with the Crystal Palace preacher preaching hell-fie & damnation ... (Oh, you traitor tube, you!) & knowing that the fire in my belly was in desperate need of salvation, i rolled rolled rolled outta bed (didn't bother to drag a comb thru my aching head) & headed for the great white throne where i communicated directly with God until i flushed my life away, away, away ...

*   *   *

As a child, i cut worms in half & watched the ends wriggle away. i poured water down ant holes to see if ants could swim. i stomped on spiders to see if it would rain. i shoved a frog down sister's blouse just to hear her scream ...

97

Didn't you?

Didn't you remove goldfish from their bowl to see if they could breathe? Didn't you toss the cat by his tail to see how he would land?

Didn't you steal candy money from your mother's purse? Didn't you smoke a cigar in the garage & throw up on your father's car? Didn't you cheat on spelling tests & swipe comic books from the corner store?

As a child, didn't you? Didn't you?

Didn't you crack open caterpillar cocoons & stunt their metamorphose?

Didn't you play doctor with your cousin behind the laneway fence? Didn't you wonder why you had what she was missing? Tell me now, didn't you?

As a child, didn't you play games with that fellow who lived down the street, the tall blond guy who bought you candy & comic books & taught you funny nursery rhymes even though you said you were too old for them ... rhymes like wee-willy-winky sucked upon my pinkie ... red rover red rover let's all dive under cover ... hickory dickory dock, the mouse ran up my clock, the clock struck one & you sucked one, hickory dickory dock ... Didn't you?

Didn't you promise not to tell because it was so much fun & he said your mamma would get upset if she knew how much candy you were eating? Didn't you? Didn't you? Didn't you ...

*   *   *

as a child, i liked to rub-a-dub-dub. i like to rub it in the tub. John the Bathtub am i come before you, come not to crucify you or defy you but to submerge your head beneath the warm, sudsy ripples that emerge when i fart & part the waves ...

... and jesus was a sailor who walked upon the water. & when he knew for certain only drowning men could see him ...

And i am your healer as i drown you beneath the water & you spout like a whale in joyous celebration as the holy spirit descends upon your head announcing your salvation ...

*   *   *

Round ball round ball pluck the baby's hair & cut it & cut it & cut it & cut & tickle under there ...

but where is under there?

i don't know. i don't know. i don't think so. i don't think you're supposed to tickle under there. i don't think i'm supposed to tickle under there. i don't know i don't know tickle under under there i don't know ...

*   *   *

who's in the tub? who? who?

*   *   *

i should be asleep ... so late it is ... too late perhaps? If he hears me awake, there will be hell to pay, and we haven't even got to church yet... They took me to church, every Sunday, my parents did. Made me think that we were here upon earth to die & meet Our Father Who Art in (Garfunkel) ...

And then there was life ... tickle under where? & then there was life ... who's in the tub?

oh Goat, then there was life ... and life became hell.

How you can remain silent in the face of all this... 'nough, 'nough, nough for today... Even if I don't let you see it, how?

7th HEAVEN DAY

So ... where do we go ... from here ... always at the start of a blank page, that's the question i ask myself. always at the start of a blank day, that's the question i ask myself. always, at the start of a blank evening, that's the question i ask myself.

so ... where do we go, where do we go, where do we go? And how will how will how will... will this get me outta here. How how how how? Need to think, to conspire, to create a plan, set a trap... I was so much better then, I'm younger than that now... how? Got to got to got to be a way to get me away....

*　*　*

why i? why You? why he? why she? why we? why youse? why they? why me? why us? why you? why youse? why them? why earth fire water sky? why body? why soul? why dust? why dust bowl? why nose mouth ears eyes? why neck? why bust? why bodily bust? why dust? why arms buttocks legs feet? why hands? why rocks mineral vegetables? why meat? why no verb? why? why why? why bodily bust? And dust to dust?

if you must, because.

*　*　*

This morning i dreamt that i woke up & looked out between my bars & was blinded by the light which was looking in on me. & there we were two duelling gun fighters at the Not-ok-Corral, face-to-face & race-to-race—and i knew (yes i knew) that there would be no backing down from what i didn't see until i saw it, until i awoke from looking out my window into the blinding light even though the curtains were drawn to keep out the bleakness of the night & even though my dreams still enveloped me, even though through the darkness of my blindness i saw nothing but the shadows on the wall, oh prisoner of the cave.

& i drew back as far as the leash would allow so as to not see what i might see if my eyes adored me but I never something something your face & grew accustomed to the light of empty nightmares so rich in texture as to be two naked Greco-Roman wrestlers making love on Persian rugs in a desert sunset while all around dark eunuchs licked there lips & wondered why it was they wished to wrestle too, only to discover they could not see, behind the clouds, the face of God; they could not feel their desire so intense & yet not there at all—a total eclipse of a total eclipse of their being which they wore like a tragic-comic mask. Whatever whatever whatever... & the face of God became the face of Satan because love hurts when day is night & water is wine & doves cry causing the blindly impotent to cover their ears in agony ... is what i did: closed my eyes & covered my ears & bit my tongue until it bled & the dove descended and shat on my head & proclaimed me his beloved & i cried out in the night, alone in the night, i cried out in the night, alone in the night & not even the echoes of the sounds of silence replied as i looked out between my window bars, over my window pain, stood upon the window ledge & leapt upon the black & white horse that galloped by, riding away forever from this place in opposite directions at the same time: all this i did & did not do this morning when i did not wake up & look between my bars & was blinded by the light looking in on me ...

and then, indeed, i woke up & wished i were dead. Goat, I think I've lost my head! Beats giving it, but oh how I miss getting it oh how oh how I love jesus Because He first loved me... he-he he-he...

*   *   *

tub ... keeps floating up ... and i think i've got it figure out ... the more i think about it, the more i'm sure that it was rub-a-dub-dub, Ducky.

Don't want to see you today, goat-ee. Wanna stay in room and suck my thumb and sulk. Why not? I'm entitled to it – 7 days and nothing, not a hint o' freedom, freedom... sometimes, I feel like, a motherless child, sometimes... clap your hands, clap your hands, she gave me clap, so I clapped my hands like iron fists upon her temples, gave her the most amusing dimples... another one that is still unsolved, sherlock.

*   *   *

As a child, simple things kept me amused. This, for instance: My mother taught me how to draw a rooster. She held my hand, fingers spread apart, on paper & traced the outline of my fingers & thumb. She then added a beak, a comb & eyes to the thumb. presto, instant rooster.

103

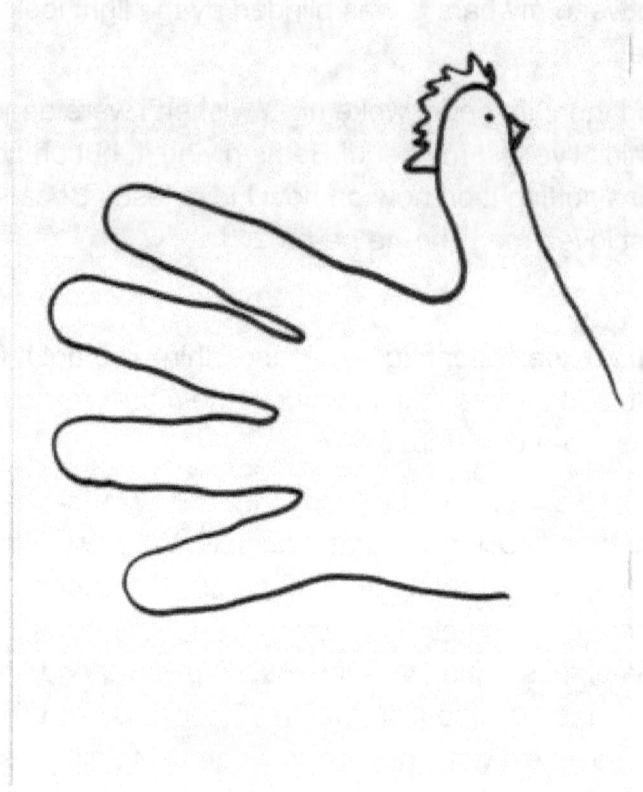

My hand roosters crowed proudly from hundreds of scraps of paper. One of them even strutted his stuff—in red, yellow & green crayon—on the bathroom wall. Another mother might have been angry, another mother might have been hurt, another mother might have been a fucker... my mother laughed & showed me how to draw a bucket of water &, with Mr. Clean & mr. sponge, she showed me how to make my creation disappear. presto. Fantastik, eh.

She laughed, Goat. Wow. Were there other times when mother laughed? None come to mind. not much ever comes to mind. Just roosters and laughter. That be it that be it.

*　　*　　*

'Half a minute ago, they were raw & runny.' (This is my ex-lover speaking as she admires her cup of steaming scrambled eggs.) 'This is truly a most miraculous thing.' (She pats the microwave & then sits down to eat her breakfast.) (what was i doing there in the 1st place? draw a bucket of water &, with Mr. Clean & mr. sponge and she and her eggs (her fucking fertilised eggs, how dare she) disappears. presto. Fantastik, eh.)

ah, but look at the inspiration—my commercial for Micro-Magic powdered Eggs: 'A true breakfast miracle!' Sold a bundle, it did. If it don't sell, it ain't creative. More creative than me, there never came ... oh how I came so creatively...

*　　*　　*

Some evenings, after dinner, my mother would slice & butter bread, cold cuts & tomatoes & make the lunch i was supposed to bring to school the next day. Then she'd leave the kitchen to do whatever it was mothers did after hours—after dinners were prepared & eaten, after dishes were washed, dried & put away, &, of course, after 2morrow's lunch was made, wrapped in wax paper, shoved in a crinkled brown paper bag & placed in the fridge.

Since i was not satiated by the fried chicken legs, roast potatoes, boiled beans, bread & butter (she loves bread

105

& butter), & apple pie & ice cream that i had had for dinner, i would, after she left the kitchen (it took her so long to leave the kitchen; so many chores to do), sneak open the fridge door—slowly so it wouldn't creak—while keeping my hand on the little button that, when released, caused the fridge light to shine (this little light of mine, i'm gonna let it shine ... hide it under a bushel, NO!) & steal my lunch &, sitting on the floor in one corner of the kitchen, would devour my salami sandwich.

And the next day, while slurping my Alpha Bits drowned in milk & sugar, i would say to mother: What about lunch? & she'd say: i made it last night. it's in the refri ... & then she'd sigh & without a word or threat, she'd cut & slice & wrap all over again ...

She sighed, my mother did. now that is something I remember.

But it sounds like a normal life, no? which is what i'm trying to say here, goat. a normal life it was. so why me? why here?

*   *   *

Ok, so seeing the goat again – made it lunch without him, before he insisted, the insistent bastard. Makes no never mind to me, sitting her before my goat and writing without talking or sitting in my room, with no goat to bray, writing without talking… not sure why here is different for goat, but if it gets me outta here and into where faster, then so be it. I'm here, I'm here, let the bells ring out, let the banners fly. It's too good to be true, but I'm here. I'm here….

*   *   *

Goat, this is good shit, don't ya think? eh? Do you know any book publishers? i mean, if i can keep it up long enough (wasn't that always my problem, not keeping it up long enough), or so she said, in her own way, that's what she said… we could go places with this ...

*   *   *

And if we've gone places with this, then where are you going with this? Where are you now? Are you in bed, naked, feeling yourself? Are you on the toilet, reading? is that you i hear grunting painfully? (Try a bran muffin.) Are you riding public transit, reading this? is the street car, subway, bus crowded? Are you standing? Try this. Turn the page ... and lower your arm slowly. (No, not the one with the book. Twit. How will you know what to do next?) Now move your elbow back and up. A bit more. More. There. Whatcha catch? Did you cop a feel. Did you get caught? is somebody yelling at you, calling you a pervert? is somebody asking you out on a date? Are you suddenly busy next Saturday night. Didn't i tell you to look before you cop? i didn't. Shit. Don't you hate instructions translated from Japanese. They always leave out something vital out. Like in my case, the vital signs. They've been missing for a long, long time ...

Ah, enjoy the ride, enjoy the read. Pervert. Schmuck… I know, I know, never insult or play down to your audience… but look at you, and look at me? how can it be – you there, me here. How so unfair…

Are you reading? Are you reading? Dormez vous. Dormez vous. i could never sing it. i could only spell it. Ding-dong-dung. Ding-dong-dung.

107

Are you in the library? Have you just come home from the library with this? Are you cheap, impoverished or indifferent? All of the above? None of the above? About to become some of the above?

Are you reading this, getting angrier & angrier? Or bored or frustrated.. go ahead, toss it mutherfucker… oh, you paid for it? Idiot! Do you want a refund? Are you asking the manager for a refund, but the manager won't give it to you because this was on sale in the remainder bin & there are no refunds on remainders. Go ahead. Complain. Gripe. Bitch. Yell… Nobody cares a shit about you, about what you're feeling. if they say they do, if they say they care, they're lying. Or they've just completed a customer-service workshop, and are acting as if they care, don't worry—it'll wear off soon & they won't care a shit about you again. I want you to know that. You need to know that. It's true. Trust me. i know that. I care.

*　*　*

Answer me this: Do you love life? Do you love anything in life? About life? Do you love your spouse or partner or children or pet. Do you love your job, your boss, the pricks you work with, your pay cheque? Do you love what you produce? What do you produce? Are you are farmer? Do you produce produce? isn't the English language funny. Ha. Ha. What a riot.

Do you love your parents or relatives or friends? Do you have any friends? Do you love making love? Do you really? Or do you just think you do? Do you fake it. Even when you don't fake it, do you wonder if you are faking it but just not aware of it? Do you know what love is? Do you want to know why i'm asking all of these questions? is this a Mensa test? Did you pass? Did you pass out?

Oh, piss off.

* * *

He spent his entire life on earth, waiting to die, my father did, so he could go to heaven. What a load. & if he gets in, then i don't wanna be there.

Glory glory hallelujah / Teacher hit me with a ruler / Met her at the door with a Colt 44 / The class goes marching on ...

But he got bored, my father did. i guess that was it. Or he got tired of living the good life & not giving God anything to forgive him for. i guess that's what happened. So then, god, he gave you something to forgive him for.

shit floats. so does ivory soap.

I don't care, Goat. i'm gonna flush it all down ...

* * *

A Pleasant Xmas Memory (or the biggest whopper yet): i was five years old the Christmas that i got a battery-operated Mr. Blinky—a toy car whose eyes blinked red & green like the lights on our Christmas tree & who, when switched on, would follow me around the house, his smile-shaped bumper beaming as his headlights blink-blink-blinked. That evening, i took my Mr. Blinky to bed with me & in the morning, when i folded back the blankets to find him, he fell on the floor & broke his bumper & smashed his headlights & he never blinked again for me ...

All together now: Ahhhhhhhh.

* * *

is it any wonder that i have never loved another? For the most part. One little fucking slip up, followed by her slipping up or fucking up when we were fucking… she agreed, there'd be no progeny. And I have not loved since, and barely loved even then, other than to say it now and again, to try it on for size, to see what it felt like or was supposed to feel like… it felt like something different, it felt like and outsider, it felt like living in america, it felt like I was living in a coffin, cough in up blood, it felt like a kiss by any other name would still be as strange, it felt like victory, but it was defeat. Like two seconds left in the game and you throw up your arms in victory, and they score from their end of the rink… (Is it possible? If it is not possible, should I edit out my metaphor for not working as (like?) a metaphor should. Wood. Chuck if a would chuck could chuck would. English. So fucked, my home and native tongue…

* * *

Shakespeare said all the world's a stage & we are just two-bit players on it—or words to that effect/affect/in fact … So what does that make actors? Are they in a play with-in a play? And what about actors in a play with-in a play? What are they? Don't even bother. I be so tired tired tired. So to be such a bother …

Now is the winter of our discontent …. I am so discontent.

Tv or not Tv?

* * *

i pricked my finger picking a rose for you & cursed. Then i remembered the crown that Christ wore & understood that others had experience worse ... in the name of love.

There are some things, i can admit, that i wish i did not know but am not able to forget. This is not in the file, Goat. You deal with it ...

* * *

Brenda was one of the many girls who joined our football team—the golden bears we were—after each game, win or lose, at the tavern on Bloor Street across from our high school, good ol' BCI. She was in grade twelve, like i was.

Brenda wasn't going steady with anybody. On occasion, she dated different players. At the tavern, she laughed at our jokes & stroked our egos, even when we had played poorly. Other girls resented Brenda & her stray-cat independent strut. if she talked to their boy friends, they got jealous & sulked & hated her.

The day we lost the quarter-final playoff game on a last-minute field goal, neither Brenda nor beer could pump up our egos, which need mega-pumping. We drank until midnight then Larry, a short muscular halfback, flashed a bag of dope & the team headed to the stadium behind our school where we had lost the game. Brenda, arm-in-arm with a couple of players, came with us. The other girls, even the girl friends, stayed behind. i could never see a conspiracy even when it hit me flush in the face-mask ...

We smoked grass & hash & a few guys even dropped acid. Larry got a football from the trunk of his car & we held a scrimmage. Brenda hitched up her mini-skirt, it did not have far to go, & played centre. We took turns at quarterback, tucking our hands between the backs of her thighs which were spread wide so she could hike the ball.

Some guys tried to tuck their hands up close and personal, so to speak, but she said: 'Hey now!' & laughed & hiked the ball hard at them.

Then Larry pulled up her skirt—didn't have far at all to lift—and exposed her white panties.

'Don't,' she said.

'it's a full moon in June,' he said.

She tried to twist away as he held up her skirt & she dropped the football.

'Fumble,' somebody called & tackled her.

'Gang tackle,' a voice proclaimed, & a swarm of golden bears descended upon her as if she were a pot of honey.

'Hey!' Her muffled voice tried to break thru the heap of losers as a huddle of hands tore loose her blouse & ripped away her panties ...

We declared her player of the Game. We thought we were conquering heroes, the way we left her sprawled and bleeding under the uprights, the football tucked between her thighs.

There were no excuses… But if asked, these are the excuses we agreed to offer: She was wearing a mini-skirt. She encouraged us. She wasn't wearing a bra. She always encouraged us. We were drunk. We were stoned. We're kids. We were losers. We were depressed. Brenda bent over for us. She stuck her pussy in our faces.

Except we didn't have to fabricate any excuses. No questions were ever asked.

We wanted her. We took her. We had her. And the girls who stayed behind at the bar, even the girlfriends? They all knew. Even the girlfriends agreed to let their boyfriends fuck brenda if it meant she got what was coming to her... And why it was coming to her, I don't know. She was fun. She was cute. She was friendly. She was vivacious. She was flirty. She was outspoken... And for that, she was gang raped?

So, where are they now, my buddies and their girlfriends? Shouldn't they be here too?

We were turds. & there was more shit to come, from me. Because there were more brendas out there—you just had to know where to look for them and how to cajole them, and how to take them down ... .

*   *   *

Give a shout. Give a cheer. For the men who brew the beer in the cellars of ol' BCi. We are brave we are bold for the liquor that we hold in the cellars of ol' BCi. & it's guzzle guzzle guzzle as the beer pours down the muzzle shout out the order of good cheer: MORE BEER. & it's just one more before we hit the floor in the cellars of ol' B...C...i!

*   *   *

why is it, Goat, that this feels like The portrait of my penis as a Young Dick?

* * *

My penis is like a puppy—spoiled, not house-broken (stirred, not shaken). Just when you think he's about to burry the bone, he rolls over & plays dead. Not even a good scratch between his saggy ears can wake him ...

My love machine is broken down. Broken down. Broken down. My love machine is broken down. it squirts ... far too fast ...

Penis. Dick. pecker. Cock. Colt 45. Louisville Slugger. Blade. Switch blade. Axe. Cannon. Mighty Thor. ('You're mighty thor?' she said. 'i'm so thor i can't even pith.') Bozo. peter. John Henry. Cunt Buster. Cherry picker. Ass Master. The Beast. Duke. Bozo. Cunt buster. CN Tower. Saggy, baggy elephant. Old Faithful. UnFaithful. Cream Machine. Bananarama. Thing…

* * *

The drunk was in desperate need of help.

Two bouncers held him; a third smashed his face repeatedly with bare fists the size of pot roasts. All because the drunk had pinched a waitress—the long-legged blonde who wore a short red skit & a white blouse with a neckline that plunged down to her navel.

There was no trial. No judge. No jury. Just instant justice. (instant justice is gonna get you. Knock you right on your head ...)

114

And i standing, behind my bar, watched fists fly—breaking the drunk's nose, splitting his lips, knocking out his teeth, blackening his eyes.

The bouncers let go of the drunk. He bled. He wept. He collapsed on the floor. He was lifted up & tossed into the street.

The waitress adjusted her red velvet panties & straightened her blouse. She bought each of the bouncers a drink. & i? i poured the shots.

2 days later, the waitress was raped in the alley behind the bar by a man in a mask... the authorities, last I heard, are still looking for me, er, the culprit, the culprit, the culprit...

*　*　*

Where were you when Paul Henderson scored the winning goal in the seventh game of the 1972 Canada-Russia hockey series?

i was in Dallas assassinating JFK.

i escaped on a lunar mission & digressed to Mars Bars, which are my favourite candy-coated peanuts, popcorn & a prize, that's what you get when you ZAP too much ...

i was in the school library making up (they say that making out is hard to do) with my then girlfriend & missed the goal. i mean, the only time in my life i allow love to take precedence over Tv & i miss out on the biggest national orgasm of this nation. i got a hug & a kiss & a hard-on for missing the game but eventually i got dumped. But then the Make-beLeafs let Henderson know he too was unloved & dumped him. So we're even, steven. Hey, what's love gotta do with it? You gotta be good to be dumped. Yeh. You gotta be good.

*   *   *

Chick-a-boom chick-a-boom don't you just love it. Chick-a-boom chick-a-boom don't you just love it. Chick-a-boom chick-a-boom don't you just love it. Don't you love it don't you love it don't you love it don't you love it ... Chick-a-boom boom ba-boom boom boom.

*   *   *

i don't write to get away from there. i can never get away from there. i write to get away from here. But once i am relocated, will i know where to go to find me?

*   *   *

Is it true, Goat, what you just asked/said/implied? If I answer 'yes' then you will… With my voice, eh… OK for this, OK… 'YES MUTHERFUCKER! YES!' ….

…ahhhhh, what a treat. what a treat. I answered 'yes' with my real live voice, sneaky bastard but it was worth it, and I am… Outside for the first time since i got here. Outside, mutherfucker, outside.

it's cool but sunny. sitting here under the lilac tree. a breeze picks up the fragrance, how nice, & daubs just a hint of it on my neck & wrists, behind my ears & under my nose, how nice. & i fall in love again remembering the fragrance she wore. the fragrance of lilacs ...

... the fragrance of lilacs ...

she wore blue lilacs, oh-oh-oh ...

shit.

there were lilacs on the table ...

they were stepping out, my folks were—going to a missionary meeting or into the missionary position ... so mama asked the boy who delivered our groceries to come over & baby-sit me. it was a saturday night. the deal was this: if i behaved, he would let me watch hockey night in canada—the Toronto make-beleafs vs. les canadiens:

and after ma & pa went out ... what did he do? he rifled thru ma's dresser drawers. he put on her silk stockings & underwear & made me wear her lipstick & dressed me in one of her blouses ...

and the breeze picks up the fragrance, how nice, & daubs just a hint of it on my neck & wrists, behind my ears & under my nose, how loverly.

shit.

we're in the kitchen now, playing man & wife or wife and wife... there are lilacs on the kitchen table. how nice, on my neck & wrists, behind my ears & under my nose, how nice and loverly... he crushed the lilacs. & other places i remember, there are places i remember in my life ... but how could there be lilacs in winter? it must be winter, no? if the make-beleafs are playing les canadiens how could there be lilacs...

I am lost in time and space. He took me on the table and there were lilacs on the table and the make-beleafs were playing les canadiens. and the breeze picks up the fragrance, how nice, & daubs just a hint of it on my neck & wrists, behind my ears & under my nose, how loverly.

117

And i know there are lilacs ... & the grocery delivery boy
has bent me over the table ... & what? where? when?
why? how? And even who (me and you, but who am I
and who are you?) & all the little details are missing ...
 molson golden, do you know what you're pissing?

and my folks come home—i'm in bed ... i hear the him
say: He was no problem at all ma'am! & he pockets his
two dollars for an evening's work ...

that was me, no problem at all.

and the breeze picks up the fragrance, how nice, &
daubs just a hint of it on my neck & wrists, behind my
ears & under my nose, how nice. even as i gag on it and
the missing details… the words that I cannot give you
'cause I cannot give me… and you had to fucking make
me beg for this, outside, and you had to sit me under the
lilac tree with anyone else but me to make me dredge
this up…

happy, goat? Buck you, buck you.

*   *   *

He said to me, ted did: Let me kiss thee with the kisses
of my mouth. For thy love is better than wine. The joints
of thy thighs are like jewels, the work of the hands of a
cunning workman.

He said to me: Behold, thou art fair, my love; behold,
thou art fair; thou hast doves' eyes. Thy lips, drop as the
honeycomb: honey & milk are under they tongue.

And i loved him. but Ted is dead.

We have a little sister & she hath no breasts: what shall we do for our sister in the day when she shall be spoken for? ted read to me from the B-I-B-L-E.

who leaves bibles in these places? god, don't people have anything better to do with their lives than work for the Gideon's and send bibles to institutions and motels ...

and Ted is dead.

As he left me for another, he said to me: Thou hast ravished my heart; thou hast ravished my heart with one of thine eyes, with one chain of thy neck.

just because i had had others! now ted is ...

*　　*　　*

By night on my bed he sought me. I sought to hide from him, under the bed where the gentler monsters were. But still he caught me ... and he prayed for me because i had been a bad boy.

my mother told him when he came home how bad i'd been ...

what did i do? break something? i knew he would come for me, he'd be angry. full of the wrath of god, or the wrath of khan ... why did i know this?

i don't know this.

*　　*　　*

The page never looked as blank as it does 2nite, Goat. Never before did i want to write words that say what i feel. & yet, what is it that i feel ... never before have words seemed so distant, felt so inadequate.

119

and even as i write & dark textures cover the page like an oil spill polluting the ocean that I am, still the page looks blank empty blank. as blank as my mind—so dark in its emptiness: like a moonless night. Ah, but what about the stars? There are no stars in this hell-sky, have never been will never be. what's that you say: How far the stars?

what shit is this?

who's speaking to me? thru me?

ah, 'tis you little sister. you have no breasts. what shall we do?

how far the stars? i don't know, little sister. why on earth would you want to go to the stars?

you see what you do to me, ted. my lover. my friend.

just because i treated you like an asshole, you had to leave. & what good did it do you? What good?

i should've been the one, ted, my lover/my friend, to die the way you did.

*   *   *

everything would've been okay forever and a day. i would've been a contented calf raised on contented milk ... but channel ZAPping began to give me headaches. i had to go see an eye specialist. He conducted a lot of tests—made me read eye charts & shone bright lights in my eyes.

This is very unusual, he said. & he asked me if i did a lot of closely focused work.

What could i say? i confessed to channel ZAPping.

Stop it, he said. You'll go blind.

i laughed. Like masturbation, no?

Like Milton, yes. He was not laughing when he said this.

so i stopped ZAPping for, oh, about 48 hrs, but soon too soon i got the urge ... & reviewed the Tv guide to see what heaven was up to.

& even though i still have my sight, enhanced by the glasses that i forget to wear, he was correct ... he was right. indeed, i have been blind forever and a day.

but unlike saul, i have not travelled to Damascus. there has been no revelation. unless this is it ... is this it? Are my lessons done, son?

*   *   *

My feet are cold. the hour grows old. i should light the light & put on warmer thoughts. perhaps i should find a pair of socks. To warm my feet. But to warm my thoughts? My thoughts of you, they more than warm my mind. They set my mind on fire. Hell fire. how far the stars? The stars are fire. they are hell ... like these thoughts of you ... hell ... all is hell... oh, heaven is a place on earth, a place called hell. Black is white, hot is cold, up is down, heaven is hell... all is hell, all is well... goat, am I well?

Day Pieces of 8

Morning has broken. Break wind. Breakfast. Fast off the block. Chip off the block. Potato chip. Potato salad. Caesar salad. Hail Caesar. Hail Mary. Mary mother of god. Mother of pearl. The Pearl. John Steinbeck ...

Diving—diving under—under water—rub-a-dub-dub ...
 First base!

*   *   *

Had a thought when i woke up. it was one of those thoughts that slips thru the fissure between dream-sleep & dream-wake, the place i hope death is like—an unconscious state of consciousness. it was one of those profound thoughts—how to save the world, save your life. it was one of those thoughts that disappears into wherever unremembered memories go forever even as you wipe sleep from your eyes saying, 'Right! Right! Yes. Oh yes! i understand.' And cannot remember what it is you've forgot.

*   *   *

All my life, i have been out of love. That is a thought i had this morning, the one I remember. Profound, eh? You'd think it would have paid me the courtesy of slipping away for ever or at least for a day. Or forever and a day.

*   *   *

i'm not doing enough (screwing enough) to get outta here. it's always how i get into & outta places. by doing &

screwing. but maybe this is where i wanna be. (home isn't where i wanna be, any more. squatters rights ended with the fire, didn't it Goat?) (the fire. the fire. i do remember a fire.) (is that why i'm here? did my love become a funeral pyre? come on baby take me higher ... am i a pyromaniac? Considering the alternatives, if that be it, it be not so bad...)

*   *   *

maybe i will simply ignore this effort, Goat, to lift me up from where i belong, from the depths to which i've sunk—the depths at which i am most comfortable. (you get used to it, you know, the depths. you get so as you're looking forward to it, the depths—sinking: where fuck all floats because the gravity is so dense. like i'm so dense. oh, the gravity of it all ...)

or maybe i will simply take my medicine because it's what you've prescribed. & if i refuse my medicine might you refuse this refuse (read it slowly; alter your pronunciation and the syllable emphasis... isn't english weird?). Might you put me out on the curb for the scavengers to ravish before the garbage people take me to the dump to the dump to the dumpdumpdump to the dump ... hi ho silver bullet may be what it takes to end this misery.

and maybe you will never discover what i have known all along but managed to forget i knew—i said nothing at the trial because i had nothing to say except words that would incriminate me even though i wanted to proclaim my innocence—my long ago long lost long ago fucking innocence—yes, i started the fucking fire.

We didn't start the fire It was always burning Since the world's been turning We didn't start the fire No we didn't light it But we tried to fight it... ok, we ignited it... there. i confessed. so set me free, Goat, won't you babe? get outta my life, now, why don't you babe ... instead you just keep me hanging on ...

what fire?

*   *   *

Deep breath & dive. Hit the water. go down under. Down. Down. Come up at the side of the pool, behind the lady climbing up the ladder (to the roof where you can see) the wet material pulled tight tight against her dripping pussy cat pussy cat, I love you, yes I due... so much is due to me and I am so overdo do-over and do it differently, goat, is all I'm asking for is the chance to do it all over again, only differently ...

maybe you will believe me Goat. i'm not innocent because too long ago i lost my innocence. this i know. & so do you. it's all written down in the file the file the file ... the one I didn't write. The one they gave you when they gave me to you...

is this what i was to find here, my file clippings?

Do you know what it's like going thru life knowing that you've never had an original thought—not even that one?

*   *   *

So. it's 9:07 and I'm not there but it's like I'm writing to you even when I'm not there, so what's the difference when I'm there and you sit there and say nothing... ok,

124

once in a while, without looking at my writing, you mutter, 'and then...' 'and how did that feel...' 'and what else...' 'hmmm... really? Dig deeper then, deeper then...'

I DON'T GET IT! WHAT IS THIS AND WHY?

How... did I get? What time is...? Here I am and you are... again, and I have no idea how ...

What have you got me on? On what have you got me? (one sentence, you fail; one you pass... right miss smythe, you idiot grade 4 teacher? Really? Language is so fucking important that one way gets you a red x and one a green check; one an f and one an A. really? Is it really, truly worth it you worthless piece of grade 4. you car in the parking lot deserved the flat... deserved the windshield wiper ripped off... deserved the busted flat in new orleans mirror cracked... only it got me, not you, 7 rears of bad luck ... but I want you to know you deserved every bit of vandalism. There are some things I make no apologies for... and had I been, what, 5 years older— first time I got hard in my hand—I would have vandalized you... the way things are going, they're going to crucify me, which I don't deserve, not one nail, not one sliver, not one whip, not one stab in the ribs... no matter how many I crucified before me, self-righteously. No one, do I deserve, but they were all so deserving, as were you miss smythe, as were you...

*   *   *

Make a list: 1, 2, 3. But what about: 4, 5. 6? & have i considered: 7 or 8?

Prioritize: 8, 2, 3, 6, 4, 1, 9, 7,10...

So my first choice then is: 8. Or is it? Well, i must choose one. (Must i? Yes, i must.) Okay then: 1. No. Wait. Well? How about: 4? But have i really dismissed: 10, 5, 9 or 2? Yes. But not: 3, 6 & 7. 3 has distinct advantages. Similar it is to: 7 in certain ways. And yet what about: 6? Oh 6 6 6 ... Not 666 ... But still could i not combine: 4 + 2? Would i not then get synergy? Or would i simply get: 6 again? Or worse yet, would i get: 6 - (7 + 3)? is that what i am destined to get from all of this: once again my only option: negative results?

it is not true that i have no choice. i was born this way. with a golden griddle in my mouth ... maybe if you believe me you will tell the others & the seas shall free me.

oh let me drown in peace. let my bloated body float to the surface & bury me on the beach. or on a couch in front of Tv which is where i'd rather be—Ontario: is there any place you'd rather be?

you know, if they hadn't cut off my illegal cable hook-up none of this would have happened. but what would have become of me? certainly nothing worse than this.

*　*　*

Legislation, administration, situation, retaliation, accusation, masturbation, big sensation, abomination, resignation, deregulation, emancipation, oh the nation, regurgitation, trains won't stop now at my station. or so says Bob Dylaniation ...

*　*　*

When i was a kid, i disgusted my folks with my eating habits—the way i shoved food into my mouth while chewing & talking. The way i shoved food into my mouth & kept it open while chewing, picking up the bits that fell back on to the table & shoving them into my open chewing mouth while talking & squishing mushed bits of food thru the gaps in my teeth with my tongue while farting and shoving. The way i burped & farted while shoving food into my mouth while chewing with my mouth open while talking & wiping my nose on my arm while sucking bits of fallen food thru my teeth. The way i rubbed my nose on my arm while shoving food into my open talking mouth while burping out bits which i shoved back into my mouth while mushing mushed food thru my teeth with my tongue while farting & licking the snot off my arm.

When i was a kid

i disgusted my folks with how i ate.

little did i know of the swollen appetites

they hid beneath their plate ...

*   *   *

is that it Goat? is this what's supposed to come up? free-verse & rhyme ... but i could so this any time ... parsley sage rosemary and mime ... poor soul, he can't chime ... hey, buddy can you spare a dime ... and this written by a man still in his prime ... who's going thru a process to cleanse away the grime ...

shall we pray? FuckFuckFuckShitFuckShitShit ...

you want me to float this one by you in greater detail.

oh yes, it's true. i remember all, all to jesus i remember, i remember all ...

oh the nights that i went to church against my will when i could've been at home watching Tv ...

2morrow, when my friends all scream about screaming while watching THE Beatles on Ed Sullivan, i'll cry. i know i will. i'll crawl into the closet & cry me down to sleep. What a cross i have to bare. At church ... while Ed Sullivan is putting on his really big shew. & i'm farting in the pew. & wishing i were any place but here.

oh Goat, how i wish i were any place but here. how do i get outta here?

if god did not exist, we would invent him.

i've got news for you, the patent on the invention of god is about to expire ...

man says god created us in his image. i say bullshit. i say man is a spectrum—opposite ends in varying degrees in constant conflict—the unequal dialectic of love/hate, happiness/sadness, pain/pleasure, ignorance/enlightenment, acceptance/denial, on/off, in/out, etc/etc—and the conflict between egotistical/humble allowed man created god in man's own image, but then claim that god created man in His own image.

so? exactly.

There's no price for admission. Just confess your sins & live a life free of sin & thou shalt reap thy just reward— thy crown of glory. Thou shalt sit on the right hand side of the Lord god Almighty praise be his name hallelujah.

What was oral roberts said? 'i need 16 million dollars or my maker (Studebaker) will call me home.' Go on home, fuckhead… but people are so stupid, they bought you life on earth…

*   *   *

Ah, the end of one mutherfucking long day… The noise in the common room is calling to me, the siren's song— Tv or not Tv? this is cold turkey. i refuse to watch if i cannot control the ZAPper. so i sit in my room, back up against the wall, & ZAP thru this because i have nothing at all, absolutely nothing at all, to do ...

Lardass, fatass, oh ye who controls the ZAPper—should i ever decide this is all in vain, that there is no ticket outta here, you're dead meat my man—even if dark & smelly cling-ons ring your asshole ...

*   *   *

just let go & see what floats up.

i'm all torn up & yet i fight so hard to stay in control ... just let go ...

need an ex-lax of the mind—free up my brain waves goodbye Norma Jean Jean the dancing machine gun Kelly aches in the belly & i sit on the crapper going bang bang, she shot him down in cold soup because i had to take a shit just as the waiter served the Lord late at night when storm winds blow my nose after dinner in fancy restaurants & i Kant The Trial The Verdict & Paul Newman's salad dressing gives me the runs ...

My love machine is broken down broken down broken down.

My love machine is broken down.

it squirts far too fast.

*　*　*

if i could direct my dreams, every night i'd dream of... I can't think of a fucking thing. Maybe dead ted before he bled. Or her before she started to puff like pastry and I huffed and I puffed and I blew her dreams down...

*　*　*

Hey, goat, last night i got fucked. The evidence was well in hand ...

*　*　*

Hey Goat, is this what it's all about: what i read in Pogo 2day: Some things you never lose, no matter how long they've been gone. is that what you're getting at? Too bad; so sad. Pogo got there before you.

But some things i can never lose.. The aroma of Mother's spaghetti sauce. Copping my first real feel—her nipple growing between my fingers as i shoved snow down her blouse. My Teddy Bears' Picnic record—a thick, black '78 I listened to constantly, until it fell and broke. My first hang-over (and my 2nd and 3rd and then, after that, it's all just a blur). Father trimming the hair around my ears because my brush-cut was getting to long. The hole in my bedroom floor—nobody knew where it came from or why it was there, but you could stick your dick in it and pretend you were fucking anybody.... Mrs. Brown You've got A Lovely Daughter. My first nocturnal emission. (eMission control... Houston, we've got a problem...). Making angels in the snow. How Frank Mahovolich dominated my thoughts the first time i made love so as i wouldn't cum too fast. (Wonder how that would make one feel, knowing people are thinking of you during sex so that that does not occur?) The last two lines of the first poem i ever wrote: 'The tree was a symbol of the world/for it was a knotty tree.' Honest Ed's. Julie's garters. Father waiting to tell me a bedtime story while i hid from him in the closet. the smell of lilacs. Riding my bicycle for miles & miles & miles & miles & miles. i can see for miles & miles & miles ... the grocery delivery boy dressed up in my mother's clothes as he had me at the table ... smelling lilacs even though it was winter ... it had to be winter because johnny bower & the make-beleafs forever were taking on les canadiens ...

*   *   *

Forever is a rainbow, a friend once said to me. & a rainbow is god's smile because when god smiles, it's forever.

a rainbow is forever, i agreed. But forever is a frown—a rainbow is god pouting. god just has pretty lips.

*   *   *

Excuse me while i kiss the sky. Excuse me while i kiss this guy.

*   *   *

My mother told me that up until grade two i was left-handed. in grade two they made me switch hands & i began to pee the bed at nights. Everything can be blame on the educational system. Everything. Look at how stupid my folks were. & they hardly even went to school.

*   *   *

Where does this leave us? Where does this heave us?
Does this bereave us? Does it Leave us To Beaver us?
Will it deprive us? Can it revive us?

*   *   *

Help me. please, help me, i said to Ted. There must be
somebody who can help me . There must be an
institution where i can go. an agency of kind-hearted
sisters of mercy who can assist me. it's best, i
understand, if i do it cold turkey. but i'm not capable, on
my own, of doing it at all. so help me please help me, i
said to Ted ... i'm hooked & i admit it ... i'm hooked on
Jeopardy.

*   *   *

Low-budgie movies, where featherless birds wear dark
rectangles over there beaks.

it's not as if i have nothing else to do, Goat ...

*   *   *

ice cream, six cents a scoop. Something else i'm
doomed to remember.

*   *   *

Excuse me goat, gotta go....

i am writing on the toilet.

(Take two.) i on the toilet writing.

two weeks of this shit? and then what? you really think
i'm gonna let you read this? then sit back & wait for your
diagnosis. for your prognosis ...

two weeks out of a lifetime in which there has been no
life. sure, two weeks, if that's what it takes. two weeks i

can surrender. You can have it. And when it's all over, you give it back to me… all to Goat, i surrender, i surrender all …

ah, that feels better… next time, though, I'm not going to wipe, then I shall sit upon the face of lard-ass…

*   *   *

two weeks in the desert. looking for a life that isn't there … the temptation is to end it all & let the vultures have there fill on this poor sucker who never had a chance …

oh yes, you think i don't know. the lazier you get, the easier it is to get lazy …

you think i didn't have to work hard to do the damage done?

i was over-drawn at the passion bank, but the bankers saw my interest & made me a loan. i went to spend my passion on you love, but you called me a dog—wouldn't even throw me a bone. so i spent it on another… say three hail marys say seven our fathers …

but why bother … because he loves you. Love me two times love me tender love me black and blue…

*   *   *

ted laughed. he didn't understand. i wasn't born this way—i had no choice … he liked to take it up the A-hole: fuckme fuckme fuck my cunt … is what ted said. now ted is rhymed with said …

we were only lonely children who became lonely adolescents who became lonely lovers … & all along, i had others … & when he found out, he said: why have i bothered to believe i love you? & he left. & i thought i

133

would never love another. (did i love him? i really proved it, didn't i?) but i changed channels ... the weather channel ... the trudy channel ... & thought, ah life ... this is it. i'm set for life ...

& when i heard that ted had died, i did not cry. & then the weather changed again ... winds coming in from all directions whipping up a dust storm breathing new life into the dust you are & ...

goddamnitall, i was not made to procreate!

*   *   *

Dear god:

2day your existence can be questioned by me—by my existence. For if i am, you are not because i am something no god could conceive unless of course god has nightmares that come true. Or unless of course you have had intercourse with the devil ... to create this hellish monstrosity: moi.

*   *   *

it was hell what happened in the kitchen, Goat. sheer hell ... but the smell of lilacs, i remember, the heavenly smell of lilacs ...

#9. #9. #9... Day

if death is dreaming forever then may i never die. i do
not wish to replay forever the dream i had last night.

outside the house without my clothes on, i begin to fly
over the Shell Tower at the CNE where father sits with
Humpty Dumpty & then i'm in a garden restaurant where
our naked waiter Adam (he has his name tag pinned to
his right testicle) takes our order & serves us the head of
John the Baptist on a sea-food platter of worms i've
picked in my back yard & behind me is the shadow of my
mother with a flashlight inspecting my asshole because
i've left brown stains on my underwear again she says &
she strikes the pose of a toreador & my father charges at
her & she stabs him with a child who holds in her mouth
a ripe banana autographed by Salvador Dali who wakes
me up to tell me that i'm dreaming & that i should fall
asleep because he's thirsty & would like me to oblige
him by dreaming that he's drinking a glass of water, so i
do, only i can't pick up the glass until i solve the riddle: is
it half full or half empty even though i know the answer: it
doesn't fucking matter when you're thirsty & my father
watches, expressionless, his face sliding around the
corner of the room, as Papa Hemmingway slips his arms
around me in a farewell embrace & we climb the steps of
the Shell Tower which bends over like a leaning tower,
only of pizza, & spills me out on fertile ground where
people & worms babble in many languages, which is
okay because i'm multi-lingual although i don't
understand a word i'm saying so i check the headlines &

they proclaim: rub-a-dub-dub tickle under there ... & the grocery boy delivers me unto evil & puts me in shit ankle deep, head first, as mother parts my cheeks & proudly plucks a worm & serves it me for supper ...

*　　*　　*

'God give me strength.' That, Goat, is what my mother used to say when i infuriated her; she said it often. What shall i say when my dreams lead to thoughts of her that infuriate me? Watch tV instead. But lard-hard controls the zapper... no problem, it occurs to me: i've watched enough Tv in my life to close my eyes & create my own show ...

ZAP... people pulling bodies from the rubble ... ZAP ... Joan Rivers interviewing Rachel Welch's bosom ... ZAP ... singing raisins ... ZAP ... emaciated children collapse on their trek to camps where no food remains ... ZAP ... a smiling Carson ridicules his ex-ex-ex ... ZAP ... rock stars cavort on the set with a VJ whose neckline plunges to infinity but then little devil-creatures try to sell me potato chips but i'm already eating twinkies ... ZAP ... a monk strips off a nun's brown habit as she licks his ear but we cut for a beer commercial... ZAP... I go for a whiz that turns into an unexpected crap (don't you hate that) & when i return, the nun has reacquired her habit & the monk is being hung by the cardinal who has one hand up the back of the nun's habit & is caressing her bare ass...

*　　*　　*

There was a hole in my bedroom floor. the hole was about the size of a hole in the centre of an old 45 record. i don't know how it got there. there was no reason for it to be there. it served no functional purpose. it just was there. i used to drop pennies down the hole. Pennies could buy you good stuff then—ju jubes, Double Bubble, black balls, wax lips. You could save five pennies & buy a pack of bubble-gum hockey cards—get lucky & get a Johnny Bower in a pack. Stuff like that. Six pennies bought you ice cream, always chocolate, in a crisp cone. Twelve bought a Superman comic book. & i never had any money, except for the pennies that my mother gave me—two or three at a time, change from shopping—which i would drop down the hole in my bedroom floor as if i were hiding my talents, afraid that if i used them i would lose them. i don't know why. it was stupid, never having any money & tossing away the only money i ever got… but to save pennies to spend? well, i tried that once. Went to the store with some of my friends & we bought stuff. I bought a little; they bought a lot. They paid for their stuff with nickels dimes & quarters & they laughed when i counted out my pennies. & so i started dropping my pennies down my penny hole…

*   *   *

The hole in my bedroom floor was about the size of a hole in an old 45. i don't know how it got there. There was no reason for it to be there. it served no functional purpose. it just was there. i used to put Vaseline around the side of the hole & stick my pecker down it & move my pecker back & forth until ... all over my pennies I'd cum. it was just the right size, & more fun than a fist.

One day, i told a friend about the fucking hole. We knew that fucking involved a stiff pecker & some aspect of the female anatomy that you could never quite see in the girlie magazines we scoffed from the variety store. when i showed my friend the hole, he laughed & said. 'Yeah but i betcha you don't really hump it.'

So i showed him. he was impressed & wanted to try it. So i let him. For a nickel. i charged my friends a nickel a fuck. & for the first time in my life, i became a popular guy. i had more friends than i ever had in my life, at a nickel a fuck.

& then one Saturday, I must've had six hole-fucking friends over & one of my hole-fucking friends told me to have a go at it, after all it was my hole. He said: 'Here's a nickel. Let me treat you.' So i took his nickel & rimmed the hole with fresh Vaseline, dropped my drawers & began to pump away. & while i was at it, i heard laughter coming from behind me then i felt cold hands on my bare ass. Rough hands grabbed my legs & spread them apart. Bony fingers spread Vaseline between my cheeks & my friends took turns ... i closed my eyes, held my breath & let the hole swallow me whole.

When i opened my eyes, later much later, & the hole released me, my bedroom was dark & i was alone. jammed into my hand, six nickels ... one from each who had used me as the fucking hole ... & one by one i tossed the nickels down the hole to join my pennies…

*   *   *

am i supposed to comment, Goat, when shit like this floats up? or am i just supposed to inhale its fresh aroma? Maybe stick my face in it and chow down upon it? What, goat, am I to do with it? And how, goat, will it get me outta hear?

*   *   *

For a brief season, never mind the reason, i was a somebody. i had colleagues. i had a lover. i hid my ZAPping addiction behind the guise of research. She bought it. i bought it. & the agency bought me for a fistful of nickels, and then some: call it a salary. & i forgot who i was who i had been. & then she said:

simon, i'm not sure how you're going to feel about this ...

... & then she found out how i felt about it ...

but our season! Oh, our beloved season in the sun.

we lived together. She seemed happy, content, satisfied. & & & so... was... i. For almost a year. & i thought nothing about the stuff & said nothing about stuff -- about the kind of stuff, Goat, that you want to see float up. Why would i? How could I think about and say about the stuff i didn't remember?

& then she said:

simon, i'm not sure how you're going to feel about this ...

... & then she found out how i felt about it ...

& I became the stuff I could not forget even though I had no memory of it...

*   *   *

Simon & Trudy sitting in a tree. K-i-S-S-i-N-G. First comes love. Then comes marriage. Then comes Simon pushing a baby carriage.

*   *   *

Every time my boss, who had taken me under his wing, said he saw himself, the way he was, in me, i wanted to under-go personality surgery.

they all thought i was like them. how did i manage it for so long? to fool them all. they looked at me & saw somebody who reflected exactly what they wanted to see: oh chameleon!

can we fool them all again, Goat? can we do it once again?

I liked my life, then. Turns out, it did not like me. no fair no fair no fair no fair.

*   *   *

Go ahead, take one last kick at the dented can of fading memories & wake up the entire neighbourhood with your primal scream.

*   *   *

i didn't fart as the class was sitting straight, our hands folded on our desks waiting for the bell to ring, waiting for the teacher—our tall, dark-haired teacher with full breasts, a thin waist & pouty lipstick-coated lips—to say: Dismissed.

it wasn't me who let that foul thunder-clap rip. But she clutched her yard-stick & said: 'Class, you'll remain in your seats & not go home unless somebody confesses.'

even though i didn't do it, i put up my hand as the tight-assed girls giggled & the macho guys snickered. i didn't do it, but i stayed behind & let her strap me ten times on each hand with the yard stick—her nostrils flared, her breath coming like the little engine that could, her breasts jiggling under her soft white blouse with the each whip of the strap.

almost every day i confessed to dirty deeds that others did. i confessed to shoving Peggy's braids in the ink-well, to throwing chalk at Larry, to setting the trash can on fire. & each time she kept me after class & strapped me harder & longer—first across the palms of my hands, and then... across the seat of my pants. & then one day, she dragged me into the coat closet, pulled down my pants & underwear, sat on one of the little chairs & bent me over her lap & she spanked my bare ass with her bare hand while breathing like the little engine that could ... until she finally made it over the top of the hill.

After that, i stopped confessing. i became the teacher's pet. & each day after class, i stayed behind to help her clean the boards. & then we'd go into the closet where our coats hung. & there she'd ask me: Were you a bad boy 2day? & i'd confess: i think i was. i think i was ... & she would & she would & she would ... little engine that could ...

*　　*　　*

Look at this pecker in my hand. it looks like what an inflated ego would look like if you could see one. it's a Popeye punching bag, the way it keeps on coming back for more. it's tragedy the way it dies; it's comedy the way it resurrects itself. But it sure as hell ain't romance.

*　　*　　*

Hey, i just had a flashback & figured this out: Man walked on the moon the same year as Woodstock. Groovy, man. Such lunacy.

141

* * *

Oh God she's coming towards me. She's gonna ask me to dance. i'm gonna shit my pants. i'll have to stand on a chair just to talk to her.

Hey, this isn't so bad. She's kind of soft & comfortable & well, she smells real pretty too.

What's the...? Get down. You'll embarrass me. She's gonna feel you if you get any harder.

Hey, i thinks she's noticed & i think she ... likes it, the way she's grinding on it ...

& then she just floated away & danced with others, left me there wet in my pants... a no-contact wet one... i never thought of her again, unit today. when she floated up while I was in the washroom soaping it up... strange, what floats up and when...

* * *

if you could see in all directions at once, you would be God. & you would laugh out loud ...

* * *

YOU deserve a break 2 day ... Mable, Black Label ... The taste of Kent. The taste of Kent ... Show us your Lucky Stripe ... Winston taste good like your cigarette should (what do you want, good grammar or good taste?) ... Take it off. Take it all off ... Try it, you'll like it ... Me & the boys & our 50 ... Where's the beef ... Plop, plop. Fizz, fizz. Oh what a relief it is ... Ring around the collar ... Mr. muscle, you're a good man to wake up to ... it's finger-lickin' good ... At Speedy you're a somebody, a somebody ... i'd like to teach the world to sing ...

When you eat your Smarties do you eat the red ones last ... good 'n Plenty good 'n Plenty ... in the Valley of the Jolly, ho-ho-ho ... Soup an' sandwich, soup an' sandwich ... the quality goes in before the name goes on ... Two all beef patties, special sauce, lettuce, cheese, pickles, onions on a sesame seed bun ... Daddy's gonna take us to the zoo 2morrow ... Candy-coated popcorn, peanuts & a prize—that's what you get in Cracker Jacks ... 9-6-7-11-11 ... and you tell two friend, & you tell two friends & so on & so on ... you'll wonder where the yellow went when you brush your teeth with ... Bubbly bubbly bubbly ENO ... mmm-mmm good, mmm-mmm good, Campbell's chicken soup is mmm-mmm good ... did you McClean your teeth 2day ... you deserve a break 2day ...

*   *   *

'Remember yesterday, when we went down to the pond at High Park & caught those gold fish?'

'Yeah, that was sure fun. Especially when you stuck the firecracker in one & blew it up.'

'That was almost as much fun as watching you swallow one. Have you seen it yet?'

'Naw i took two shits since, & it ain't come out.'

'Wonder where it is.'

'i don't know, i drank a lot of milk. Maybe it's still swimming around inside my belly.'

'Yeh, like Jonah & the whale, only you're the whale & the goldfish is Jonah.'

'Shit yeah. Hey come on into the laneway.'

143

'What're we gonna do there?'

'i'm gonna see if i can make myself puke, & spit up Jonah.'

'All right.'

Kids, eh. And yet, so innocent. Why not stay that way? Why grow up and become this way? I mean, so a few fish die. Better than what happens next.

* * *

Because i hear my teacher say 'Never start a sentence with the word because' i ask her 'Why?' because I'm a shit disturber that way. & she says 'Because i said so' & that's all she says because that's what her teachers have told her because it's a rule that generations of teachers have found too difficult to explain to inquisitive children because the rule is bullshit, which is why my teacher doesn't have an answer to my question which she, as a child, never asked, which is how she became a teacher, by not asking questions, which is how fundamentalists become fundamentalists & ignorance breeds ignorance, because people are afraid of asking questions & even more afraid of answers to the questions they dare not ask…

& she also said 'don't use run-on sentences, simon!'

* * *

i think therefore i scam.

* * *

And in the end, what remains? My remains. So disgusting even the vultures turn there backs on me. They forsake me, God's creatures do. if i were a bone (or an actor out on loan) they would at least have the courtesy to pick on me ...

*   *   *

Mother's angry. She's really upset. She wants me to fall to my knees & repent. She's got out the wooden spoon to strap my behind.

i mean, after all, i'm goddamn thirteen years old, you can't strap me mother. i'm too goddamn old & no, i won't stop swearing at you, you goddamn fucking witch bitch.

i mean how was i too know? Every spring she turns the mattress over. Who would have thought? i mean, it seemed to me to be the perfect place to keep my girlie magazines.

& even though she's yelling at me, at least she is speaking to me.

*   *   *

there's something else there, in my anger. as if my anger is a mask. a mask for what? for hate. but why would i hate her. & yet that's what i feel, as i sit here with nothing to do but feel ... hate her i do ...

see, goat, you've been good for me. I'm in touch with my feelings... do I get a free pass for that?

*   *   *

suffer the little children? no, we make little children suffer ...

don't they see? can't they tell? everybody sing along: oh the circle is unbroken ...

*   *   *

what is it exactly that we're after (forever after) here? is it clemency we're after here? or proof of my insanity? but have i not already been proven sane? If so, then why am I here instead of Kingston penitentiary, or Graceland in Memphis Tennessee? a poor boy like me.

i was daddy's travelling companion long before i was ten years old. we said grace together. i got down on my knees & he got down on his knees behind me & ...

so calmly i write this wrong.

you think i don't know it? but what does it prove? where does it get me to know this & confess it? do you think it was ever so far below the surface? do you think it was something i could bury anywhere at all? there's not enough dirt on me to bury what daddy did, what mama saw—it was against the law, what daddy did what mama saw & turned her back on ...

Float to the surface? Fuck me, it was never under water! But for one brief moment way back when… what's the point, unless it's meant to get me outta here, somehow. unless it's meant to set me free ... yes, that must be the case. i'm writing for hope. if that's not the case then there is no case at all ...

*　　*　　*

i remember this picture from one of the girlie books i kept stashed between my mattress & box springs. it was a scene from a movie. i forget who the actor was. But the actress was Gina Lollobrigida. You could see her breasts—most of one, & all of the other, including HER NiPPLE! Could heaven be better than this? Gina's nipple to masturbate too? Oh joy. What fun. What bliss. What an erection. What an orgasm. My first famous nipple & it's mine forever frozen on the page ...

and then ma finds the magazines & calls me a sinner & threatens to tell daddy ... & i freak knowing what she knows and is about to do, and does, after she beats me with the wooden spoon. She gives him licence to do what he's been doing all along, in the name of god... & you you wonder why i hate my mother ...

*   *   *

you know, Goat ... you don't have to be a native child sent to some boarding school run by priests. you don't have to live on the rock, be part of the flock, an altar boy blessed after hours by his priest. you don't have to live in a foster home, live in a shelter, live in the streets. No, you don't even have to leave home ...

a little house, with a little back yard, with a little garage with a little car in it. with little rooms & little cupboards & little closets. & such little people with their little religion & their huge repressions & their sick little little minds ... I knew better; I know better. But they... they all... they all got the better of me, and I of others even though I knew better, know better, am no better...

*   *   *

and the night comes on. it's very calm. i'd like to pretend that my father was wrong. but you don't want to lie to the young ... no, my father wanted to lie with me. but now my father is gone. i saw him die as i closed my eyes. he's gone & there's nothing more to be done. & my mother, she was never any fun ... did my folks ever

147

have fun ZAPZAP ... the smell of lilacs ... a spring day ...

i came home early from school ... the lilacs on our street were in bloom (oh, Goat—i had a gut-wrenching tummy ache & i came home early from school ... shit floats, Goat, it's true ...) & i came in thru the back door (we had lilacs in our backyard too—the smell of lilacs) & my mother was in the kitchen on the table ... there was a vase on the table with fresh-cut lilacs in it ... the kitchen was alive with the scent of lilacs.

& there was a shadow over her, my ma ... the grocery delivery boy ... over her naked body ... on the kitchen table ... his ass swaying as if in a breeze & the smell of lilacs & my stomach in knots ...

my stomach, Goat, in knots ... my mother yelling but not fighting ... no, not yelling ... not yelling at all ... she was, what? Not yelling at all, but sort of like, not in fear or terror…

when he baby sits me & dresses me up like mother & takes me on the kitchen table he says: if you tell, i'll kill your mother ... & i believe him, oh Goat, dear Goat, i believe him & what's worse ... i want to tell because i want him to kill her ... but still i say not a word ...

& i held my breath as he did what he did & i imagined the smell of lilacs as i disappeared beneath my bedroom floor & counted all my pennies & took them to the store where i bought wax lips & ju jubes & bubble gum & hockey cards—all johnny bowers & my make-beleafs forever ... until he was done with what he was doing, i hid beneath the floor, inhaling the sweet scent of lilacs in my make-beleaf garden ...

Day 10, the big fat hen

Am I doomed to spit out words like a punch drunk boxer who has lost his mouth guard spits out teeth ... or shit out words, like a hypochondriac who has over-dosed on prunes shits out ...

stuck in the verbal outhouse i am without a Tv to ZAP or a magazine to read or to use to clean up my mess ...

are you satisfied Goat: i shit my pants. & the orderlies have locked me in—of course i was cursing & screaming. what the fuck do they expect. alone with myself—and i hate myself. of course i'm going to argue with myself ...

but i'm not done with this shit, am i?

*   *   *

Here with you; there without you. All feels the same. I don't get it. You are driving me fucking crazy… mind you, when not with you, nothing compels me to continue. & yet, I am so compelled to continue… what is this hold you've got on me? you've really got a hold on me. and yet say you next to nothing, which feels as if it says so much…sad songs, when all hope is gone, sad words say so much… they reach into your room… Turn them on, turn them on… Goat, why don't you tune in and turn me off?

Just feel their gentle touch… there is no gentle touch…

i stood in the kitchen & i shit my pants. & my mother opened her eyes & acted not at all surprised. 'Oh simon,' she said as she stepped into her skirt. & the grocery delivery man disappeared into the shadows. 'you're home early simon. you're not well?' she said. 'Let's go lay down ... '

* * *

turn the page.

start with a fresh page. rip out the page. use the page to wipe away the shit that has floated up & turned my memory into something other than this hellish place where i am now, lost in time & space—reliving my hell ... still living in hell ...

wipe the slate clean ... start all over again. i've got to forget everything i have remembered—it's the only way to escape from this hellish dream ...

it was all a dream, Goat. it was all a dream. nobody shot j.r.—nobody fucked me from behind, nobody fucked my mama on the kitchen table. the smell of lilacs means shit to me.

* * *

He scores. He shoots. & nine months later he's faced with the threat of a paternity suit.

instant replays show an offside pass began the rush, but the referee—out of position on the play—allowed the goal.

She claimed a deliberate attempt to injure on his part should have resulted in a misconduct. He swore she should've been penalized for hooking.

The siren sounds & the game is over, ending in an aborted tie. But the ice has been broken & the donnybrook continues, long after the last spectator has left the arena.

*   *   *

This is what the Goat said to do. He said: Write it down. Write it all down as it comes back to you. Even the lies. And this is nothing but lies. It's the lies I despise, so I put them all down as I make them all up. that's what makes me the best copywriter at _____. You should see the size of my bonus. Makes up for the lack of the size of my thing, trudy doesn't say to me, to nice she is to say such things to me...

There are times, as i write it down, that what comes up is something soft & warm & sweet smelling. something like normal. the trouble with normal is it always gets worse ...

normal like this: My friends & i spent a lot of time in the laneway behind my house on _____ Avenue. there we played tag & ball hockey & hide-and-go-seek (only we called it hangle-seek) & we played SPUD & red-light/green-light & dozens of other games. & there we built go-karts & tree houses & snow forts & cardboard forts. & there we became friends and mortal enemies... we friends fought & ended friendships forever, only to make up the next day & swear allegiance forever more to each other, blood brothers—spit & blood in the palm of our hand, mash our hands together then lick the mash to show that we were more serious than serious. to show our oath was true.

what is truth?

& in the laneway behind our homes… there we smoked cigarettes when we were ten. & we even smoked a cigar one day that somebody had swiped from his ol' man. there we smoked together & grew up together & threw up together. god, how that cigar made us sicker than the flue in the dead of winter.

& there we looked at girlie magazines together— magazines that we swiped from the corner variety store by hiding them behind the comic books we bought. yes, there we studied the naked female form & felt ourselves grow hard in the place that we thought was meant for pissing on frogs and in streams and down ant hills. & we touched ourselves & showed off ourselves, & sometimes, late on a summer evening, when hardly anybody was around in the laneway behind the house were i grew up, we touched each other ...

there, we swore at each other & swore at our mothers & fathers & made each other laugh as we cracked jokes & knuckles & belched & blew the foulest smelling farts you could ever imagine and could never inhale for fear of death and yet we exhale so we could take deep breaths of each others foul farts, that is how much we loved each other as only kids are capable of doing. Our farts, they were like a diary of all the meals our mothers made us eat.

chicken fart coming.

here's a mortadella sandwich.

mashed potatoes & peas.

who had baked beans last night?

cabbage & pierogies coming up.

heaven help us. not cabbage & ...

but god would not could not spare us from the stench that we inhaled like metaphors escape me now...

& there we were brave enough to dream. we dreamt of who we were & who we were gonna be. & brag? how we did brag. & lie. we lied about who we were & who we were gonna be. & who are parents were & what they did & how much they made & how much allowance we received & how loudly they screamed at us & how badly they beat us. & no matter how rotten we made them sound, we defended them. & no matter how rotten we made them sound, we could never make them sound as rotten as they were—because they were our parents & they could not love us as much as we desired to be loved: & so we learned how to hate ourselves, how to prove we not worthy of the love our parents were not capable of giving. even the parents who might have been nice. they were the worst. because you really had to lie to make them who they were not.

except ...

i had to lie to make mine sound ... normal. or i would have been laughed out of the laneway.

no ... it was not all a dream. it was not all a dream ...
(stay on track, let this pleasant smelling shit continue to float up—leave the vile turds behind ...)

& there & there... & there we compared heroes.

richard's my favourite.

richard sucks, you traitor. he's a canadien. mahovlich all the way.

you think mahovlich is something. he's an oaf, that's what he is.

i wanna be ferguson.

fuck you, i'd rather be eddie shack any day.

Keon all the way.

Over richard? Or beliveau? How retarded are you?

take away horton & baun & the leafs would be nothing ...

give me a break, bower makes the leafs great.

that sieve?

you calling bower a sieve? you're gonna pay for that!

so normal, in our secret places—behind garages, up trees, in basements ... such bravado. such lies. such silence about all that was real—about all that hurt. we never talked about anything that hurt. maybe we didn't know how to share pain. maybe we didn't know it hurt ... if you fell & skinned your knee & saw blood, you could see that it hurt, whether you showed it or not ... but the pain inside? how could you know about what you can't t see?

& even if your best friend almost takes out your eye with a broken hockey stick & somebody asks: are you okay? does it hurt? you would look at him as if he were a whimp for asking and say: *Get off my ass.*

maybe that's were it starts, that men don't talk about pain, in laneways & back alleys. maybe that's were the lies begin to feel like truth. glorious truth. the lies that set us free from mundane pain ... that grows inside like cancer ...

i don't know. i don't fucking know. & even now, i don't know if any of it is real or not. it's just there. like a scene thru a window. or is it a painting?

what's going on? what went on? what remains to float up besides more pain more pain more pain ... what a pain this is, a pain in the ass ... a pain in the ass ... that's who i was as a child—a pain in the ass. i deserved every hurt i got because i was a pain, Goat, who should've never been born.

don't you think i don't know that? do you think i need to be reminded of it here?

oh Goat, why won't you answer me? whose idea of therapy is this anyhow? you think i don't know what this is?

itHURTS. itHURTSitHURTSitHURTSitHURTS.

*   *   *

You know what? Goat bites his nails. i can tell. i suspect he was a bed-wetter too. Maybe still is. i could detect, beneath the odour of cheap after-shave, the faint smell of urine. a smell i'm familiar with, having pissed myself on more than one occasion—having pissed myself almost every evening of my childhood. little red riding hood. chicken little. chicken pot pie. pot head. dead head. gratefuldead ... will be grateful when I'm dead ... dead ... dead.

The smell of urine never leaves the body of a bed-wetter, no mater how many showers you take or how you try to mask it, lone ranger. i know, kimosabe. don't i know. it gets trapped in those tiny little pores and infuses your nostril hairs & it remains there to haunt you every night of your life ... even the sweet scent of lilacs in the spring cannot displace it totally.

*   *   *

there are places i remember, in my life, like my parents' bed—a big double bed. a warm & soft & sweet smelling place.

a place with pillows, lots of pillows, & soft flannel sheets. a place i could hide in, feel safe in. a place where i could take my sunday afternoon nap. a place i could explore when bored & discover warmth & darkness between the sheets as i travelled from the sweet smells of cologne & after-shave that permeated the pillows to the stale smell of nylons & unwashed feet at the foot of the bed, passing over a musky scent in the middle of the bed—stale farts & sex.

stale farts i knew. but the smell of sex? i shouldn't have known the smell of sex then, Goat. i shouldn't have known that smell. but i did. only i didn't know it was sex. i only knew that, in their bed, was a familiar smell—a late at night smell, a pain in the butt smell, a father saying prayers with me smell, a grocery delivery boy smell, an excited grade school teacher smell ...

i can detect it anywhere—that vile stale musky malodorous smell.

*   *   *

but this day is dedicated to normalcy, not to pain or hurt or anger ... watch me...

156

in the brown bag of penny candy i bring home from the corner variety store, i have an assortment of jaw breakers, black balls, Lik-A-Maid, Jersey Milk bars, pixie sticks, wax lips, pan pies, licorice cigars, Popeye cigarettes, bubble gum hockey cards, jelly baby mummies, sponge toffee, marshmallow bananas, Double Bubble bubble gum with Pud cartoons, Bazooka Joe, licorice whips, shoelaces, twisters, Pez, Rosebuds, Peps, Thrills, Juicy Fruit, Chiclets, jujubes, spearmint leaves, Coffee Crisp, Aero bars, Kit Kat, Humbugs, MacKintosh toffee, fruit drops, wine gums, candy kisses, Hershey kisses, mellow rolls, candy cones, Smarties, pink elephant popcorn, Cracker Jacks & Sweet Tarts.

And in the summer i add a selection of popsicles, icicles, fudgicles, ice cream bars, Eskimo Pies & Nutty Buddies which i eat while standing in front of the open refrigerator so that the cool air will minimize the melting.

see? Like any child. Normal!

*   *   *

and after i cut her & fled our house, which was a very, very fine house, with two cats in the garden, I used to have a hard on… and fled our home and native land and fled our home & broke into the vacant house that I remember like I'm living there now even though I was living there then, when he was alive, and i crawled into the closet, where i discovered warmth again, as i pulled musty coats off hangers & wrapped them around my shivering body as i flashed back & heard my father who art not in heaven stomp thru the house fee-fi-fo-fum looking for a the blood of an englishman……..

but how come the house is empty? this much i know—
my father is dead. i saw him dying on the couch at the
old lady's house. but where is mother? does it tell you
Goat, in the files, where my mother is? where have all
the flowers gone? does it say why the house is boarded
up? can you explain why it looks as if judgement day
came & the house was vacated in a twinkling of an eye?

my father is dead. my mother is gone. the house is
boarded. there's nobody home. & in the closet, i
rediscovered the comfort & security of cloaking myself in
the invisibility of darkness.

& as i shiver myself to sleep, i wonder if daylight will ever
come ...

she left, didn't she, my mother did. when? why? How???
How did she get out of there? My god, she got out of
there! Save yourself, mama. Run mama run mama run.

*   *   *

The Man from UNCLE. The woman from AUNT. The
nephew from NiCE. The niece from NOwhere man living
in her nowhere land maybe she's a bit like the lesbian
from Lesbos, the gay from Gator AiDs, the transvestite
from Transylvania, the Hare Krishna from Hades, the
Oral Roberts from cunnilingus, The Billy Graham from
the Three Billy Goats Gruff, the bird of paradise from
Shangri-la, the Green Giant from the Valley of the Jolly
ho-ho-ho ... the lint from my navel as i gaze into the
tunnel ...

The advertising executive from the horse's ass ...

The separation of church & state. The separation of my
parents. The reconciliation of Jim & Tammy. The

election of Ronald Reagan. The ordination of a Polish Pope. The loneliness of the long distance masturbator. The end of the world. The lint of my navel ...

*   *   *

—Warp speed, Chekov.

—Captain, we can't. Ahead. A flock of ... Seagull.

—You mean seagulls, Chekov. As in Gertrude & Heathcliff.

—Sucked up the rear vent, Captain. Fucked up our warped speed completely.

—That's warp, you meathead.

—Aye, Captain.

—That's Scotty's line you half-wit.

—Snotty's line? Snotty's little softy?

—You're a little softy, Chekov. A little softy in the head.

—Well then, Bang, Captain.

—Bang what?

—The gun on the wall. in the first scene. it's got to go off, sir.

—There was no gun on the wall, twit. Besides, this is the first scene.

—in the cherry orchard.

—What fucking cherry orchard?

—The one owned by the three sisters of mercy who took us in even though we had sinned against God & nature ...

—There were only two sisters, Chekov. They were sluts & we barged in on them. Came uninvited, we did, with a bag of goodies & a bottle of wine & we got it on that night.

—That's illogical, Captain.

—That's Spock's line, Chekov. Besides, what's so illogical about it.

—Exactly.

—You mean ...

—Go ahead, sir.

—Spaced out ... the final frontier ... & i don't remember what comes next.

—Or when you came last

—That too, Chekov. That too.

*   *   *

Me. i'm it. i am the one, the only barrier to completing my work. But what is my work? what have i tried that's worked? What have i tried that hasn't worked? What have i tried? Not much. What haven't i tried? A lot. Who's tried me? Almost everybody. Who's on trial? Me.

but i refused to speak.

if you say anything, i'll kill your mother.

i think she's dead. isn't she? but i didn't speak. she left, i remember. but that was a long time before my father disappeared—or was it after? & i got taken away somewhere. to a home, not my home ... this world is not my home, i'm just a pissing thru ...

how long ago—i'm ZAPped in time & space—can't date anything: never dated nobody until you, trudy... when did we float apart? Why did we float apart...

*   *   *

Before i got here, before Goat sent me into this war, sometimes the absolute only thing i wanted to do, the only thing i could think of doing, was to watch Tv.

And jerk off.

the all & only thing i wanted to do was to sit on the couch, channel changer in hand, & watch the tube. No matter what was on or not on.

Oh, i preferred it if there was a dirty movie on, especially something foreign where i could make no pretext of understanding, or something with a famous actress in it even if i only got a brief peek at her tits. Sometimes, as i watched, i'd tape with my VCR & then, during commercials, playback the naughty bits. Of course i taped all the beer commercial & the gum commercials, because the women would be almost as naked (and better looking) than in a late-night, soft-core flicks ...

& whenever i wrote my commercials, i made sure there was as much naked flesh as possible showing—soap commercials were my favourite ... & i slept with all the soap actresses ... even while i was living in love ... living my lie ... if she hadn't said

simon, i'm not sure how you're going to feel about this ...

oh, how I used to feel about you... if she hadn't said, and if she had found out about the soap commercials and all

161

the actresses in them who fucked me so I'd re-suds them in the next soap commercial... we were supposed to be in love, trudy and i... that was the best I could do, trudy... if you had known how bad my best was, you would have been the one to flee. You would have never thought you could have him or her or it, with me. not with me.

& here now, as i tire greatly of this here now, i want to do what i used to do—only i have to battle the asshole who controls the common room (the romper room, so child-like he & his cronies are). i do not deserve to be here. i do not deserve to be here. this is punishment. this is hell. let me at the Tv. give me the ZAPper.

*　*　*

i had a girlfriend once, for about three minutes it seems. Whenever she was over and we were around my folks & we wanted to talk dirty, i'd ask her if she'd heard from Virginia & she'd say: no, not for a while. i think she's with Dick ... & then we'd giggle.

Or she'd say: Yes. i heard from her just recently. She says she misses Dick ... & then i'd know that we should find some place where we could be alone together—a laneway, a garage, an empty church gymnasium—because she wanted it & i wanted to give it to her.

Silly adolescents. But like I said, that lasted about 3 minutes because I could not last even that long... and so she fled, like trudy should've...

*　*　*

Something funny happened to me on the way to my lobotomy ... but i can't remember what it was ... i can't

162

even remember what night it is ... but i remember friday nights and baby blue on the tube—no need to zap. Pure porn soft and simple, for almost two hours. And there be me... all I need was like not even three minutes. But I'd be in for the whole show and often it would come back and I'd get another three minutes with me and baby blue...

Friday night. i sip & write. Cheap wine to nurse my appetite & bleed my ulcer dry. Painful regurgitations distract my imagination. My crooked fingers slither across computer keys as if taunting an Ouija board. They strike, pause, strike. Tap out interrogations. i who once presumed to fly, how is it now i barely crawl? Good question. To which there is no honest answer. & so i dawdle. Clear my throat. Wipe clean my screen of fingerprints. Pick my nose. Scratch my crotch. Delete the inquisition that precedes my flashing cursor. Sip another sip & gurgle. *Oh flashing cursor, are you the role i assume 2day?*

Hark the herald, muttering obscenities beneath his wheezing breath. An old man with burnt-out eyes who reveals himself to children playing in the park. (Yes officer, the frantic mothers say, you would recognize him anywhere. Such a limp, such a shrivelled thing.) indeed. There is nothing here to fear. Not this vestige of impropriety. There is no poison in my sting. No sting exist without first a bite. (To think that once i munched on apples.) Shall i gum a peach to death? Let the juice dribble down my chin or leg?

Oh devolution. Oh bitter defanged hiss. From this petty life of grime is there no absolution?

Move closer love who art in heaven, or wherever thou may be. Examine this eczematous portrait, my ghostly phosphorescent image. Has-been i have become. Never-was i've always been. Sluggish snake shedding yet another skin.

Oh cold cruel cross, where is thy redemption? Your suffering, it was in vain. Your curtain-call, your last refrain, revealed a fraud medieval. The heavy stone, eternal burden, remains in place. Unsaved and uncomforted, we suffer still.

Oh modern age, you bear Caduceus boldly into battle. Debunk miraculous misconceptions. Transplant the heart. What does it matter? You feed the world as well as you resolve the riddle of the soul. My vegetable love, uncultivated, withers on the vine. i gag on wonder bread & acerbic wine.

The king is dead. Without successor named. Sex, drugs 'n rock & roll remain. See how my skin has yellowed, love. Watch the layers flake away. Like faded memories distorted. Like bellies that are bloated. Like un-expiated lives discarded.

Send me a crust. A crumb. A morsel that i may ingest more than indigestion. Or send a dog. Yes, send a dog to lick these wounds. Oh send a dog for i am in search of paws to scratch a match. To smoke an illicit cigarette. Though nothing refreshes any more. Not even reflections of your lips, love, upon this weathered snake who in the face of love burrows deep into his cavity.

What name now for love? i ask.

Oh milk & honey. Oh promised land. Oh bloody turd. Oh cold bed pan.

On my belly dare i crawl thru silver needle's squinting eye? i am not a rich man. Neither am i camel dung. All the same, i rehearse. How i rehearse. For bon voyage in royal hearse or on an ass. Yes, mark me down an ass. Hey, hosanna. Who hosanna? There are no throngs to greet me as i arrive at journey's end & ask: Just where have all the flowers gone? As if they've been there all along.

& in the end, a rubric i request. A modest epitaph. Perchance Memoirs ... Bah that will not do. Pretentious. Dull. & so untrue. Perchance FOREVER YOUNG ... Hah. Oh red-eyed psychedelic fantasy. My ulcer sings discordant harmony. i toss the dog my final bone: RAMBLiNGS ... We like the sentiment, the certain dithering connotations. A senile rolling stone, i gather moss. Attract flies. Am something my landlady can despise.

oh how we used to rock & roll. No more. The flame it flickers oh so low. Night is now a silent time in which i pay for crimes that have not paid. indeed, the nights now cost me plenty.

What cowardice, what abject fear, keeps me bolted & confines me here? Are these questions not rhetorical? Like that? & that? Or are they rather allegorical? Like two divided once by three the answer is eternity. The beast.

Yes, it's Friday night & all that means. Or used to mean. it's all so mean. was it so cruel of me to leave, love. To leave unshaven & unforgiven. To leave you cut & bleeding.

Before whom now shall i make amends? & for what shall i make amends? My ignorance? & with whom now shall i lay me down to sleep? The answer? it is in the making. Or is it in the undertaking? Ted is dead. Trudy too. & what within her, unsurvied.

How late the hour grows. The hour it is late. & after the winding down of real-time clocks, what whispers of immortality remain? My oracle is silent now. After predicting endings so predictable from the start ...

My tongue is dry. My tongue is dry. Tragedy is in the severed union: breath given once to life is too soon taken from your lips. Allow me, love, to ingest another part. Dust, my love. That's where i'll start ...

*   *   *

& then i moved into my old home and bought a Tv and hooked up the cable illegally & was quite content to live happily ever after ...

but the cable company unhooked my hook-up. and I found myself on the move again. To where? To when? On the move again.

*   *   *

it's snowing again. Will my life ever end? Now is the season ... discontent.

Winter was the season of my discontent. i hated that January weather. Relentless. And February no better ... That's what i hated about it. Day after day of snow and cold and cold and snow ... And everybody bundled up.

Shapeless. Nothing to get excited about. Nothing to keep me warm.

But then, here comes the sun. Little darling, it's been a long, long cold winter. Here comes the sun. All right! And the wraps would peel off under the glare of the sun. And fun fun fun, until mummy let my daddy go away ...

DAZE Eleven ... blah blah blah ... heaven

My grade seven French teacher kept potted geraniums on the window sill of our classroom. One sunny days, we closed the blinds & tied the blind cords to the stems of the plants. She came in & muttered something in French & pulled the blind cord & swoosh, up went her potted geraniums, dirt spilling all over the place, & down we went, the entire class, to the office. She didn't last the semester.

See, cruelty. We all have it in our jeans.

*　*　*

it was about a week after i left her & ran back to my home sweet abandoned home, that i heard a knock on the door. i was feeling low, dragged out hungover & tired & i figured this is it, & decide to go out without a fight, so i answered the door.

there was a door-to-door funeral plot salesman on my door step. Without blinking an eye he said: 'good day sir, have you ever thought about your family's ultimate future? would you be interested in protecting yourself & your family against inflation by investing in a personal plot 2day? if so, i'd like to take a few precious moments of your time to explain ... '

i told him i thought it was a great, what he was selling & if he'd come a week earlier i might have bought. the problem was, i explained, that my family, my wife & three kids had just died in a car accident & they were already buried ...

You could tell, it was marvellous, that the man had never thought about death before, the way his face went ash white & then a sickly green & he fainted as i shut the door on his foot which was buried deep in his mouth.

*   *   *

in grade one, they discovered that i was left-handed so they tied my left hand behind my back & made me do every thing with my right hand.

They made me go to for recess that way, my left hand tied behind my back. On a winter day in January, with a packing-snow-fall falling, they sent me out there with one arm tied, i.e. only one are free ...

Target practice, that's what i became. Target practice for every bully & whimp in the school, from grade 1 to 6. Even the girls, who were not supposed to cross into the boys side of the schoolyard, came over (red rover red rover let every mother fucker come over) to take their best shot at me, or to just watch & laugh.

So here it is, floating up: i shit myself. i was afraid. i shit myself. And do you know what those fuckers, the teachers, the socializing agents of the system, DID??? they made me wipe clean myself with my one fucking useless withered branch of an arm. Those sinister assholes, made me wipe myself with my wrong fucking hand.

& why are they not here?

*   *   *

The photograph in the chest in the basement ... GOAT! The child who looks like me with the lady i had never seen before ...

the child is my father (who art not in heaven) and the lady ... the lady who called me over ... as he lay dying ... oh god, oh goat ... she's the lady in the picture! My grandmother! my father's mother!

he had always said ... his mother was ... DEAD ...

why goat? why? what sin had she committed against my father ... what sin had he committed against her ...

the lady in the photograph was the lady in the house where my father lay dying on the couch ...

another lifetime ago, when i got a phone call from a lady who said, 'your father is dying ... & i said: .Good.. & she said: .That's not very nice.. & i said: .He wasn't very nice.. She said: He's changed. & i said: Death does that to people. & she said: He wants to see you. & i said nothing. but i took down the address.

& when i came to see YOU, more out of curiosity than sympathy, i was shocked to see that where dark waves had once crashed upon your head was a dead lake of dull grey. & for the first time, i really looked into your eyes. Under the yellow film & cataracts i saw a hint of green. Yes, your eyes were green once, like the sea. Like the sea. Like my eyes.

& even though you didn't recognize me, you were so sick, i recognized me in your eyes & i was sick, sick, sick.

& the lady said: 'get him out of here. i can't take care of him. i don't want to take care of him. i never wanted to take care of him. i'm too old to take care of him. besides, you were right about him. He isn't very nice. take him away.'

And i was sick. all over the floor. 'Shit,' the lady said. 'You're as bad as he is.' And i fled.

and that night i dreamt of the sea. i dreamt of drowning in a stormy sea. i went under once. i went under twice. i looked for your hand to hold on to, but no hand was offered. i went under 3 times and never resurfaced.

i dreamt of crosses. carrying three rugged crosses into a cave. erecting the crosses in the darkness. crucifying me, myself & i on the crosses. & shadows lit bonfires beneath my feet and I was consumed by flames ...

& i woke up with my flaccid pecker in my hand and sperm all over my belly. & i knew that the king was dead. & i wondered if the king would ever live again.

*　　*　　*

& i hear my mother's voice. i have no choice. fresh smell of lilacs.

- franky, can you bring my groceries in?

... and deliver us from temptation, for thine is the kingdom & the power & the glory ...

... & he helped her bring the groceries in ...

... & on the kitchen table ... Mable black label ...

& i came home early form school ... & you put me to bed & held me because i was crying. & i inhaled it on you mama: i inhaled the stale musty smell of sex ...

& you swore me to silence & i did not betray you ... instead, i began to suck my thumb. & daddy put pepper on it to stop me. instead, i began to pee the bed. & daddy put a clothes peg on my pecker to stop me ...

*   *   *

Normalcy, goddamnit!

i was the perfect copywriter ... english major, psyche minor, raised on Tv, detached & restless. What does it matter anyhow? i could write exactly what the target market needed to hear, because i couldn't care less about them or about myself. What does it matter? What does it matter?

What does it matter when you're living in hell & don't know it? What does it matter when you're living in hell & can't feel it burning ... what does it matter when you're madder than a hatter & hell feels like home sweet home sweet home ...

*   *   *

i found love in the shadows. No, not true. i took love into the shadows. Forged love in the shadows. Forced love into the shadows.

Only you wouldn't call it love. i did.

i had my own way to love. My own way to roll. My own way to do those things that were good for my soul.

*   *   *

172

Last night i dreamt about Johnny—Johnny Bower. He was naked & maskless & the Montreal Canadiens were scoring on him at will, against his will. that was all he had to defend himself with, his will. he was deserted by his defence; non-existent was his offence. & i leapt over the boards at make beleaf Gardens to help him—i leapt over wearing rubber boots & lugging my broom: the rubber boots i wore on the ice of grenadier pond; the broom i used to defend my net against enemy forwards who buzzed around me like killer bees.

& i could do no better than Bower. I could offer no help, no resistance.

Like father like son.

*   *   *

i had always thought of myself as a stellar goaltender until the day i came up behind a group of my friends standing around a picnic bench at high park smoking cigarettes & lacing up their skates. i was about to say: 'Hey guys, bower's here!'

but i heard one of them say: 'Do you think Simon's gonna show 2day?' & somebody answered: 'who? rubber boots? Would it make any difference?' & they laughed. & somebody said: 'That witch couldn't stop a beach ball with his broom.' & they laughed so hard they choked on their smokes.

so i turned away & walked home, walked the dozens & dozens of blocks home from the park. walked home alone in the snow. & i never played again. But i wanted to play, Goat. i did. But how could i, knowing how they felt. But damn it, i wanted to play so fucking bad.

it hurt so bad, worse than anything (anything!) else in my life, it hurt THAT FUCKING BAD, goat. More than ANYTHING.

i thought i was good. it was the one thing i thought i could do—stop rubber pucks on the frozen surface of grenadier pond. i thought i could & i thought they knew i could. & i thought they wanted me there.

so i walked home & hid ... in the closet ... even though my father wasn't home, I hid in the closet because that's where you go to bury your shame.

*　　*　　*

last night, the make-beleafs lost to the Jets. another sad game not worth paying attention to. it's not like it used to be more than 20 years ago ... before Sergeant Pepper even. i remember those Leafs as if 2day were yesterday, all my troubles seemed so far a way. Now it looks as if i'm here to stay ...

i can probably put Punch Imlach's team back together, if i wanted to ... The owner, Stafford Smythe. Coach & General Manager, Punch Imlach. His assistant & friend for life, King Clancy.

in goal, wearing number one because he is number one, Johnny Bower, the maskless wonder ...

Those were the days when Tim Horton, Allan Stanley, Carl Brewer & Bobby Baun provided the defence. When Red Kelly, Dick Duff, George Armstrong, Bob Nevin, Ron Stewart, Dave Keon, Bob Pulford & Frank Mahovlich provided the offence. & Eddie Shack provided the entertainment.

And now? Who cares. Some are dead. Most are forgotten. Some are in management. Who cares ... it's too early in the a.m. to give a shit, but not to take one ...

*　*　*

does a bear shit in the woods? you bet. & i am an animal. A mammal. A circus bear, Born in captivity. A bear in winter. My instinct is to hibernate always. Yet i must perform.

i have been declawed by those who manipulate me. 'Do this,' they say, 'and you shall be fed & housed & clothed.' But shall i be set free?

My teeth, once sharp, are dull. My senses, once sharp, are dull too. My instinct is weak, as weak as a blade that cannot cut thru butter melting in the sun.

i cannot distinguish between friends & foe, fee-fi foes, even though i suspect i have no friends. Only foes here & everywhere. Like bars, they cage me in.

How shall i be set free from this ignominy? & even if i were set free, would i survive in the wilds? would i remember how to shit in the woulds? would i be set upon & slaughtered by other beasts, my remains left for vultures to pick over. Or would even the scavenger vultures turn away in disgust?

*　*　*

i am the egg man. i am the walrus. There are places i don't remember, in my life ...

*　*　*

There must be a God. Here's proof: i have a joint. it was smuggled in for one of the dull-witted animals by one of

175

the disorderly orderlies. i traded a pack of cigarettes for it.

Look at it, fat & well-rolled: just waiting for a match to light it & lips to suck it.

Breath 2-3-4. it's what i want. it's what she wore 2-3-4. Or didn't wear. No underwear. 2-3-4. Beneath the palm leaves spreading out picnic shade 2-3-4. Shall we ants? itch itch. Scritch Scritch. Make romance. Like doggie doggies. Where did doggie doggie doggie come? Rude doggie doggie humps your leg & then you rub his belly & then you have him doggie doggie ... doggie style doggie. Doggie doggie ... doggie gone. Dog gone it in the closet with the closet clothes you wear & skeletons you leave there 2-3-4. there must be god: smoke is proof. But can you smell that i am stoned again, naturally 2-3-4 ...

first time in oh-so fucking long time & time here does not exist here see it's already noon here and I don't see goat today until afternoon & my breakfast has grown cold dear, like Paul Revere here & the British & the British & the British are coming ... & we fire our guns & this ain't no picnic, no, with ants in my pants ... not ants, no, but hands, hey who ... breathe 2-3-4 ... inhale 2-3-4 ... remember nothing 2-3-4 ... forget everything ... 2-3-4play ... in play ... afterplay ... game we play ... round ball round ball cut the baby's hair & cut it & cut it & cut it & cut it & tickle under where? under there ... but where the fuck is there?

*   *   *

i'm tired. i'm moping. This is dull. i'm still in a sweet-grass daze ... & every few minutes i have to go tot he can to let my ass drain ... oh institutionalized buggery!

it's not getting me anywhere, this writing, least of all not out of here. i don't want to write. But i am. Sort of. Writing.

i'm waiting, Goat, for you to call me in ...

* * *

Hey Goat, afternoon to you... Your Gestapo guards (so-called orderlies; more like dis-orderlies) are perverts. i've got the scars to prove it. But do you care as you sit there?

Fucking assholes. Fucking my asshole just because they smelled the odour of the ganga gods emanating from my hole in the wall of a room...

Am i surprised? Should i be? What proof is there, except for the blood & that could be caused by almost anything, right? like self-mutilation. they're pigs, these guards.

What rights do i have? i'm here because of what i'm accused of doing & the people who's job it is to keep me here are doing unto me... there's no fucking justice, or difference between us except there's is institutionalized buggery condoned by the state & what people have accused me (how do they know; what do they know) of...

i mean, here you are conducting tests on me ... & you make me write for my freedom. but when i lay me down to rest, with a sweet grass high, they take me and make me ... & at night, when i lay me down to sleep in this hole in the wall, they go home to eat their spuds & vegetables & meat & wives & kids & dogs & cats ...

tell me Goat, who's crazy here? Who? Who? who? Are you?

& it's all because they smelled the grass. can't escape from reality here. if you try, they will give you a reality more horrendous than the reality you are trying to escape from ...

you can break my body but you can't take my mind. you can break my body but you can't take my mind. you can break my body but you can't take my mind. you can break my body but you can't take my mind. you can break my body but you can't take my mind. you can break my body but you can't take my mind.

besides, no reality you inflict upon me can be more horrendous than the reality i'm capable of inflicting upon me, myself & i ...

what choice do i have but to remain silent. they have the power they do, my prison guards. guards? guards my ass.

what choice did i have but to go back ... to go back to where it was dark: the closet of my existence ...

*   *   *

i'm thinking about our front lawn. it was the size of a welcome mat, it was. But father kept it trimmed & mowed & edged. & every spring, from the little border of brown earth, there would bloom a splash of colour—tulips. A celebration of spring, of innocence.

this time remembered is science fiction. So unreal. But it was there, i remember, before things fell apart ...

i remember building snow forts on that little scrap of lawn that was covered by pillows of white, day dreams of white.

How small i must've been. How large the snow forts seemed. i could bury myself behind the walls & nobody could ever find me there, lost in my dreams of white—so warm no matter how cold it got. it's where i want to be. There again. White & innocent. Before the thaw & things fell apart ...

i am thinking of a picture of me i saw in a family album once (a family album, HA! Oh pretentious normalcy.) i must've been maybe six or seven. it was one of those pictures, four for a quarter, taken in a machine in a mall.

i look like a marshmallow boxer, you know the type—the guy who's guaranteed to lose the fight to advance the career of some rising star. i am holding both fists in front of my face as if to say i'll take on all comers. But not quite completely obscured by my fists is a crooked frown. if you study it, you'll know my bravado is a pose.

i am not a fighter. My fist are not dangerous.

You see, i was the kind of kid who liked to strike poses, i wore each one like a mask, hiding my true self: i was in training—learning how to obscure any semblance of emotion, learning how to counter punch with cold lies, learning how to withdraw into myself & not feel any of the blows reigned upon me. Not feel a thing... Not feel the lump in the lap of the man. The lap upon which i sit. The man who sits just behind me & my crooked smile, back far enough to be out of focus & obscured by darkness, but never-the-less in the picture.

The man. The man. The man.

Oh how things fell apart, but i felt nothing as it happened.

*   *   *

And then one day, Goat ... i had a cold, & father, not mother, came in with the Vick's Vap-O-Rub, only he didn't rub it on my chest where it was supposed to soothe & ease my congestion, no. That's not where he rubbed it at all. & what was i supposed to do, Goat, because he was father & i was son. & i trusted him as he rolled me over & did not soothe my congestion ...

*   *   *

You can pick your nose. You can pick your friends. But you can't pick you family.

So why did you pick me goat, and why do you do nothing with me? you just sit there as if performing a lobotomy by boredom… sit there and grunt a few what? statements of encouraging even though you know not what I write here? You have nothing better to do, goat, but sit there as if… as if this is supposed to be or do something?

Time! Time gentleman, please. Time to go back to my hole… and where do you go, my goatee?

*   *   *

i don't want to write. This has become too much like work. i'd rather be eating. Popcorn or potato chips or a peanut butter & anything sandwich. i've got the munchies & i'm not even stoned, any more.

A joint. A joint. My confessions for another joint.

or Tv or not Tv ... Tv would truly satisfy me ...

*   *   *

Heaven is better than this. Oh boy, what joy & bliss. i'm gonna walk those streets of gold. i'm gonna live & never grow old ...

Oh boy, what bullshit.

But let's face it. Heaven is a crap shoot, right? i mean, even if it's there, which it isn't, the place has got to be as dull as a carnival midway on a rainy afternoon after you've spent you last quarter on stale caramel corn & you've got not a cent left over for a drink of anything.

So is it any wonder that christians are sinners. They know where they're going, if they stay on the straight & narrow: dullsville. But hey, let's face it, who wants to spend an eternity on the midway when all the rides are shut down because it's sin to have fun. so heaven doesn't look very inviting.

so the christians stray. You better get your licks in now, while you're mortal—you can always pray for forgiveness from your sins & ZAP ... thou shalt be forgiven. What a deal! What a deal!

& if you're going to stray & feel guilty about it, then damnit, you better stray far to make your guilt worthwhile, right? & then ask for forgiveness so you can die and go to dullsville... What a deal! What a deal!

*   *   *

i remember once hearing my mother say to a school teacher: you'll have to excuse Simon. He was born prematurely.

And 2day i wonder, can you die prematurely? To die prematurely implies that there is a specified time that you should die & that, if you were to die prematurely, you would've died before that specified time ...

Can you ejaculate prematurely? To ejaculate prematurely implies that there is a specified time that you should ejaculate & that, if you have ejaculated prematurely, you have ejaculated before that time ...

Think about it on my behalf please, Goat. i have better things to do, even if nothing is what i have to do.

i heard mother say to a friend as they sat around the kitchen table drinking coffee, i heard her say:

He didn't want to stop, you know. Not even after he began to teethe. He wouldn't take to the bottle. He wanted his titty. & he bit, you know. He had these two little sharp teeth protruding thru his gums & he'd clamp on to me with them & suck & bite until i bled. & then his father would get upset, because he was a tit-sucker too, you know ... i mean, aren't they all. i'd tell him i was too sore & he'd get upset & curse the child. Men. such pigs. it was all rather silly, really, but then that's when he changed. i'm not sure what i even mean by changed, but he did—Sr., that is. Not that i minded, because he left me alone for long periods &, well, you know how i feel about it with him ... i don't know ... i guess it was because Simon was born prematurely, you know, that he didn't want to let go ...

that's when he changed. & you changed too, ma ...

you let the grocery boy deliver you from salvation ...

but what was his change? was i his change? for i am a jealous god ... god, the father, was jealous ...
 vengeance is mine, sayeth the lord ...

get down on your knees simon. let's pray together. you are a sinner simon. sin is painful. i am here to deliver you from pain.

get thee behind me Satan.

or is it that satan is already behind me ...

so Goat, we have a motive, yes?

*　　*　　*

The best job i ever had was during a brief season of relative peace after i left the agency, and her...
answering the phone for Happy Days Escorts. We advertised ourselves as an AC/DC service, and I wrote a new slogan for the service: Happy Days for straights or gays. That's what I said when i answered the phone. Cute, eh. Sometimes, though, for variety, i'd say, 'Simon here. Straight or queer?'

People phoned just to hear my voice. i got my share of heavy breathers.

& my choice of clients.

*　　*　　*

Writing copy for the ad agency was like ... Like what? Like being sentenced to a minimum security prison for

183

life. i showed up, i put in your time. &, at the end of the day, they let me go home. Big deal. Sometimes, i had to serve weekends. But I did it—proved i could belong. Proved i could be normal. But always, under the surface.. Like constant tremors before the big quake hits ... before the volcano erupts ... i knew ... But for a season (in the sun, me and joy, we had fun) i forgot who i was. until she reminded me. and then, and in the end. The love you give is less than the love you take...

*   *   *

They grew old. They grew old.

Last time i saw my mother, on her bread was mould.

Last time i saw my father, he was naked. At the end of his bed his trousers were rolled. his mother wanted me to roll him out of there. he had always said his mother was dead ...

she's dead too, you know, my mother.

*   *   *

i was in grade two, i was. i remember not much more than a lot of stomach cramps. i always had to shit shortly after i got to school. To relieve the stomach cramps. i don't know why i couldn't shit at home.

one morning, i got to school & the teacher decided to not let me go because i asked to go every morning ... & so i shit myself & after that she let me go without question.

& one time a big kid (he had failed grade two the previous year; that made him a big kid in our class) followed me down the hall & into the washroom.

The toilets had no doors & he stood outside my cubicle & laughed at me as i sat doubled over in pain & grunted to get it out. he laughed at me. He was a big, skinny twerp with red hair & freckles. & the next day he was their again & after i took my shit, he crawled under my door, knocked me off the toilet bowl, got me in a head lock & stuck my head into the water & into the shit & blood that i had crapped ... & he laughed as he flushed the toilet ... & i thought my head was going to go down the drain with the crap & blood ... & then he wiped my ass with his hand & smeared my shit all over my shirt ...

is he in here, Goat? is he? where is he? He ought to be here, goat, but he is not, goat, his is not...

i didn't shit for two weeks after that & i got sick & they took me to the hospital, my parents did, & the doctor gave me an enema & i finally exploded ... & after that i shit in the lane every morning behind my house, before i went to school ...

*   *   *

I am lost in time and space. I am losing the human race. I don't know what, I don't know when, the big fat hen... One, two, buckle my shoe. Three, four, knock at the door. Five, six, pick up sticks. Seven, eight, lay them straight. Nine, ten, the big fat hen

So, Goat, what the fuck am i supposed to do with it? what am i supposed to do. i am what i am? but i ain't no Popeye the sailor man. i'm more like Wimpey. Whimp the jailer man, keeping myself in this prison of... Goat, you tell me. What do i do with a memory of having my head shove down a toilet bowl, flushed with my shit? Of having a prick wipe my ass with his hand? Or with remembering father stuff or mother stuff? Am i cured by remembering? Can i now go forth & multiply? is this my ticket out of here? is this my ticket out of all that i've been? & if so, why do i want to jump the night nurse, ram my rod into her every available orifice & hump her & pump her until i bump her ...

What point this, goat?

You don't have to have a point to make a point, do you?

* * *

Tell me why-y-y, she cried. & i said there ain't no reason, there ain't no reason ... As she bled from her belly; held her guts in with one hand & held out the other, asking me why?

* * *

Tin soldiers i hear them coming. 4 dead in Ohio. 21,000 babies may die this year form preventable diseases. How many more? i love the news. it makes me feel almost human by comparison to whatever is reported ...

Hey Goat, did you here the news 2day? Oh boy. 14 women shot dead in Montreal ... shot by a man like me only he used his gun not his pecker. How many more? How many more? if he hadn't finished himself off in the ultimate ejaculation, would you have made him my roommate?

What would happen if i turned my pecker on myself & shot? it's loaded, you know. Only i can't reach my head ...

How many more?

* * *

The light at the end of the tunnel is what i see when i bend over real far & kiss my ass god night, irene. irene good night. God night irene. God night irene. i'll rape you in my dreams ...

*   *   *

That's what i am. The least of what i can be. Oh Goat, wouldn't you help me?

*   *   *

'You know what you're problem is?' a teacher said to me in grade nine. 'You have the attention span of a kid in kindergarten. i'm not here to amuse you. You get no toys or nap time here.'

i said: 'you know what your problem is? you're a fucking creep.'

& he slapped me across the face, in front of the entire class. & i repeated myself & he slapped my other cheek ...

Later that day he was repairing a flat in the parking lot, wondering which of the kids he had abuse had gained revenge.

Later that week, he was cutting his cat, which was strung up by the neck, down from the rafters in his garage. & he was left wondering which of the kids he had abuse had gain revenge.

Later that month, he was calling the fire department & rescuing his family from a burning house, wondering which of the kids he had abuse had gain revenge.

Later that year, he was in an accident because when he pumped the brakes of his car, they didn't work. The accident report showed that the brake fluid had been drained from the master cylinder. & he was left crippled with plenty of time to wonder which of the kids he had abuse had gained revenge.

Later, repeated later, I gained my revenge...

*   *   *

'there is life in the desert,' trudy once said. 'you just have to know where to look for it.' this was before we were living together, when i was serious about myself & forging a career. this is when i had forgotten all that you want me to remember.

i wondered why she said this. but i didn't ask her. we were having lunch at a rather posh restaurant. i don't recall the exact conversation that led up to it. i was taking business, animatedly. As if it meant something. As if all the fucking business in this entire fucking world means a goddamn fucking thing... & she just said it & stared at me, as if she were seeing thru the mask i didn't know i was wearing. Staring thru and looking for the life within.

there was a nervous moment, and then i said: 'yes, you may be right. & if so, what are the demographics of the desert?'

she laughed, picked at her salad, shook her head & said: 'you are impossible, but i love you.'

& i thought, i love you too, but said nothing. & she accepted my silence ...

how long before the fall was that?

life in the desert. Where to look for it.

i couldn't get the line out of my head, like trying to clean the sand out of your shoes after being caught in a sand storm.

Exactly where do you look for it? is what i should've said. where is life? show me life. prove it to me, damn you ... prove it, that we have life in this desert, so I can live it with you, is what I should have said. (now that ted is dead, is what I would have never told her.)

There was hope then. Not with ted. Oh, I loved him, but did not know how to love. Nor did he. But that is what 12 years in a bizarre school will do, where they separate you from your parents and language and culture and life ... where they all but take you life and if they had, you would have thanked them for doing so, or so he told me in one lucid moment long ago and far away ... no wonder no wonder. For too long I wondered how I could love him and he not me ....wonder no more, not after he told me his story, so sorry about your story, Ted, but we each have our stories and I would not share mine with you, and now you are dead, and I wonder no more, and there is hope for hope no more ...

But there was hope with trudy. I knew, for a season, how to fake love. And she was a reason for me to do so... and then she said what she said and hush-a hush-a, we all fall down.

*   *   *

hello memories, you're not my old friend ... underwear ... under there ... where is under there ...

ah, goat, my life is nothing compared to the institutional abuse, the obtuse abuse, of church and state that takes place every day in every way, it's not getting better and better ... the institutionalized creeps and perverts on government payrolls and blessed by the divine, like it's all fine all the time all fine ... suffer the little children to come onto them, and they will be ripped from end to end ... I am nothing, no thing at all compared to them ... I am who I am and am not much of that by comparison – an amateur I am ... that does not justify one iota, not one, but then this is not a justification. It just is. Unsanctioned. As it should be. Bless me father, compared to the sins of your people, I am a lamb at the slaughter ...

i swear this lamb did not touch her & make life hell. i swear. please, believe me. the devil may have done it. i cannot say what he did or did not do to me. but i swear if he made life hell for her i was not his accomplice. no. hell no. on this one, you can be sure. just because i didn't know, doesn't mean i did what i did not know, does it? just because you shoved my head into the shit-filled toilet bowl of my existence, doesn't mean i did what i still don't know ...

i don't remember her ... & even now i'm still not sure ... tell me no. hell no. did i even ever have ... did i even ever have a little sister?

NO! hell no ... fuckhellfuck no no noooooo.

12th day

Here i am again, goat. Today and then two more days, and then? And then? Freedom ... freedom ... clap your hands. Clap your hands. Freedom ...

There were no dreams last night goat.

That's a lie. The night was full of dreams. i just don't remember any of them.

That's a lie. i choose not to remember any of them.

That's a lie. i choose not to tell you about them ...

*   *   *

Looking out my window bars, i see the sun shine & it feels like the first time i have looked out my window since i got here, not that i can remember. & if i cannot remember looking or not looking out my window, how can i be trusted to remember anything at all? especially those thoughts last night, thoughts that could have been my imagination falling into or out of the cusp of dream state.

Even now while i am wide awake (at least i think i am therefore i am): i remember my father taking me swimming one summer day in Dufferin Park. just me & my father. Where are all my other friends? At cottages. At Wasaga Beach. Or on Lake Huron. Or on Lake Simcoe. Or. Or. Or ... anywhere but here, not imprisoned in the city by summer.

i didn't want to go into the wading pool, even though we had walked a dozen blocks to get to the park. There are other kids there, others who have not escaped the city. They are with friends and siblings and having fun. Together. Laughing. Together. Laughing at me. together. And i didn't want to go into the pool alone, where they were. Together.

My father didn't understand. He just looked at all sorts of other kids there, playing there. He didn't see them as pairs or groups or flocks. He just saw kids playing and he said: go on. & i said: no. and he said go and i said no, you can't make me.

& i started to cry & my father said: 'what are you crying about? stop crying, simon, or i'll give you something to cry about.' but i wouldn't stop crying so he gave me one helluva a swat across the ass, & then another & another & another ...

Then he dragged me all the way home. & of course, i cried all the way home. & my mother wanted to know what the hell had gone on. & my father tried to explain that he had, one time in his life, tried to do something with his son & that his son had proven there was nothing that could be done with him.

& i crawled under my sheets and cried myself to sleep in my arms. & i don't remember father taking me anywhere again. Except to church. Every Sunday morning and evening ...

don't you see, goat, you can do whatever you want from monday to saturday as long as you go to church on sunday and confess your sins because jesus loves you, that's what my old man said. and jesus loves to forgive, so we give him so much to forgive us for, for which to forgive us. For.

I don't understand goat, if not going in was a sin, for which i needed forgiveness for, but i prayed for forgiveness for it, and it didn't work. My father, who aren't in heaven, he took me nowhere fun again. nowhere fun ... i mean, he just wanted to take me for a swim, & i let him down ... & he hated me for it. Forever, he tried and i did not, could not, would not ... . i just don't understand. Me. him or Him. Them.

*　　*　　*

why don't you all fade away, become somebody else's memories. become a movie that i watch and cluck my tongue at.

such a bad movie, how could such bad actors act so poorly. like who is that sitting there in the back of the theatre—don't you hate movies about movies—giving head to winos: fifty cents a head. what a bad actor sitting there in the back row, the dark back row as the skin flick flickers—the breasts and chests and cunts and cock and sweat and breath all flicker as the winos move in one by one and pay their quarters in advance and he gives head like you would imagine the angels from above would give it if they traded in their angelic voices for deeper throats.

Who? Who is? Who is it, even when he is giving head. And the coloured girls sing ... .

*　　*　　*

Your problem, Simon, i remember a teacher telling me, is that you're never serious. As she spoke, you could tell

193

by the look on her face that she was deadly serious.
Now, however, she's just dead. About that, i am serious.
Although i had nothing to do with her death. On that,
trust me.

Actually, i read about her death in the newspaper. Then
June Callwood wrote a book about her.

The teacher's problem was, that as a teacher, she was
always deadly serious. Then she quit teaching and didn't
lighten up. But did some good deeds. So when she died
people wrote nice things about her. And eulogized her.

i think she died from being deadly serious, about
everything. Even her seriousness.

*   *   *

i found love in the shadows.

No, not true. i took love into the shadows. Forged love in
the shadows. Forced love into the shadows.

Only you wouldn't call it love. i did.

i had my own way to love. My own way to roll. My own
way to do those things that were good for my soul.

*   *   *

if i say i can't continue, will you let me go?

i can't.

i recant.

i Kant.

Let's face it, sir, the objective reality of my situation is
known only in so far as it conforms to the essential
structure of the knowing mind. So didn't i blow your mind

this time? Didn't i? & if you don't mind, what you know is who you know. & you now know me not as you presumed me to be but just as i am i come to you & say, People in here just gotta be free ... . if you could read my mind, love, in the shadows ... i could've been a revolutionary or a poet. but instead ...

But i can't free you. After all, only objects of experience may be known whereas things lying beyond experience are unknowable. So unless you've experienced me, you, as you claim i've experienced you, can't know me & i can't know you, beyond the proven facts which you can't deny.

Oh, i see. To know know know me is to hate hate hate me. & you do. Well i hate you. Yes i do.

isn't it a pity. isn't it a shame. But, you must admit, there are things-in-themselves that can be neither confirmed nor denied, but are known. Such as God.

Sorry, i can't buy that.

But if you Kant then how can a moral code be know.

Exactly.

You mean it can't?

i mean Kant thought it could be but i think (therefore i am) it can't (therefore you ain't).

Exactly. To you. Because if it can't be known, then you can't be free. Check ...

Shit.

... mate.

*   *   *

Why am i so nervous. These are only words. & they're not true. i do believe i owe these words to you ...

* * *

My best friend & i, we could be the only hostages left in this sauna-city, held captive by the summer doldrums. But we don't care as we sit in the school yard shooting marbles across over-heated asphalt that steams like breath in winter. We don't care as we suck on purple popsicles, gulp ice-cold Coke from squat, green bottles & crack jokes about dumb-ass teachers & goof-ball kids gone to summer camp. We don't care as we make each other laugh with gale-force bluster. Like when i break wind as he takes a swig of Coke. & he howls so hard he can't swallow the fizzing soda which escapes thru his flared nostrils. Doubled-over by hysteria, i almost pee myself & can't save my popsicle as it slip-slides off its stick, slops upon my grimy shorts & drools cool rivulets down my tanned legs.

Our guffaws echo off the school's brick walls & overflow the fenced-in yard before we declare 'Truce!' & resume our marble war. Then he lets lose a protracted belch & we hoot & roar again, oblivious to the storm clouds gathering overhead until the deluge breaks & heaven shocks us with electric bolts that short-circuit our frivolity. But we don't care as we skip home thru muddy puddles, playing tag & dare, looking like two swamp things emerging from the belly of a misty bog.

We don't care that our marbles are forgotten—left behind on cooling asphalt: Mementos to mark our passing. We don't care. No we don't care. innocent friends, an arm around each other. Cheerful comrades, plotting future escapades. We don't care. No we don't care.

Unaware of the historic cycle: Just around the season, fall.

My best friend & i ... now Ted is dead ... he was the only one who understood ...

* * *

How is it i'm supposed to remember what it was i did that got me here when my mind's come loose in time & space.

... in grade four ... was it grade four? how can i know. Peter Small -- was it PS? Whomever he was, he was the only kid in the school who was slower than i was. The only kid i could beat up because he couldn't beat me up. The only kid who was too stupid to know he didn't have to take it from me. he didn't know, if he had said: Lay-off creep! ... i would've crumbled.

it's gym time. We're outside. Track & field. Who thinks this shit up? Hop-skip-and-jump. i'm running towards the sandpit. PS dashes in front of the pit & kneels down like a dog on the tracks. it's something we do to one another. it messes up the jump, but the jumper is supposed to leap over the person in his path & try not to land face first in the sandpit. i mean, there's no competition here. No medals or ribbons to be won.

The kids on the side-lines are all laughing because PS has never had the nerve to do this. it's like he doesn't trust kids to leap over him. He's like a dog that's been whipped so many times that he shies away from a hand that reaches out to pet him ...

197

& i ran him down. Hit him in the head with my knee. Knocked him into the pit. Landed on him with my full weight.

i didn't mean to hurt him. (Yes i did.) i didn't mean to make him cry. (i sure as hell did.)

& all the kids called me asshole. They helped Peter up & tended too him.

what about me? what about me? what about me?

i was angry & wanted to fight him, but i knew i'd have to take on the entire class because they had taken his side, just because i ran him down.

i'd been looking for PSs all my life. Weaker than me. Frail. Fragile. Vulnerable. i've been looking, not to apologise to them, but to take them out, knock them over. Hurt them good.

i mean, what about me?

*   *   *

i almost beat it you know, all that i was & all that i've become.

becoming a revolutionary or a poet was too tough an assignment, though, like something that might demand some semblance of commitment on my behalf—so instead i became an advertising copy writer ...

just like staying with her ... demanded to much of me ... . all my life, searching for

Candy is dandy. But to stick her is quicker.

& i became a lost soul wandering in the wilderness searching for other lost souls to rob of their birthright. i took away the drop of water they were saving for a desert kind of day when they might need a bead of liquid to quench their thirst. i convinced them that they weren't really all that thirsty & seduced them into spending money on mirages in the desert ...

*   *   *

tell me it's a mirage ...

rub-adub-dub ... tickle under ...

he's too old to bathe with her ...

*   *   *

believe it or not, every sunday they went to church, my parents did. sunday morning & sunday evening. they would pray for us & for themselves & for forgiveness.

two times every fucking sunday. there was a lot they had to ask forgiveness for ...

*   *   *

Hitler must've had quite the system. i've been at this for a lifetime & i'm no where close to six million or six hundred thousand, or six thousand or six hundred ... okay, maybe six hundred ... nah. 6ty? 6? 666. aye. Aye, that.

*   *   *

Beware the ides of march, the tides of march, the rides you can go on in March, the march hares in your nose when it blows 'cause you're about to take off your clothes & rake off what goes with whatever was said before this, this this & that, which is exactly where i'm at as i sat on the stool where i sit, so i can shit before i shave then shower, more power to you ... i hope they don't screw you. Amen. ah men ...

* * *

i mean when you consider it is all for nothing anyway, you should be surprised that i was as good as i was, considering how bad i could've been ...

* * *

he's too old to bathe with her ...

it's saturday. always on saturday. i have to take my bath before i can settle down on the couch to watch the maple-beleafs forever play the canadiens or the red wings or rangers or black hawks or bruins ...

'what's a bruin, daddy?'

'i dunno. get me a beer.'

when did he start drinking?

when did she arrive? little ZAP ...

rub-a-dub ...

what the fuck is going on here? what's going on ...

Who is ... ? What is ... ? Where is ... ? Where are ... ?

every saturday, before the hockey game, my father rounds us up & puts us in the tub ...

us?

Rounds us up ... us? We? Who?

us?

* * *

'mommy,' i ask one saturday when i'm in the kitchen getting him a beer. isn't daddy too old to take a bath with us? she's doing dishes, running water. she doesn't hear. or pretends not to. it's all right because i remember what he said:

'this is our secret, simon. don't you tell anybody & i won't tell anybody what a bad boy you are; what a cry baby you are. if you tell anybody simon, you'll go straight to hell. do you want to go to hell?'

i shake my head no no no no want to go no no no ... but it's not to hell that i don't want to go. That would be a relief compared to compared to compared ...

rub-a-dub-dub three in the tub. & who do you think they are? god the father. god the son. but who's playing god the holly spirit?

Us is more than us two us ... us is, who the hell is us?

*   *   *

Have i confessed enough to ya, Goat? Don't you see my true colours coming at you? Can't you fine tune the reception with what you've got?

Every morning i wish that you would come & take this away, like a chamber maid coming for the chamber pot.

How do you think i'm doing, Goat? can you smell me now? have i started to rot? or do you even bother to think of me? do you think i'm doing fine? Fine enough to soon be set free?

i'm doing bullshit. i'm doing doo-doo. Cuck-a-poo-poo. That's what this is. The biggest turd of all. Don't go rubbing my fucking nose in it, Goat. it's been rubbed there before.

Herd me away from here. Or ask me to my face & i'll tell you: Nothing is what i remember best of all. Nothing is best remembered.

* * *

The president of Romania fucked his children & had himself video taped doing it. Why ain't here in here, for fuck's sake?

* * *

Get thee behind me Satan & pump away.

* * *

Ah, you say, but he's dead, the president of Romania? So what am i? Chopped liver? i'm worse than dead. They keep me alive. they keep me revived. They make me reconstruct my own videos in living nightmarish colour on the big screen of my mind. & no matter how hard i try the channel zapper, i'm stuck on this arid channel without cable—i get one station & one station only. & this fucker is it.

* * *

i read once in a psychology text that you become the one you hate. I am turnips.

& you Goat? you're so far away from me. you send me on this journey with no support or supplies except this pen & these sheets of paper. sheets not good enough to wipe my ass.

well, you can eat it.

you have no suggestions for me, do you Goat. you have no advice. & if you made suggestions, would i listen? & if you gave me advice, would i heed it?

None of this is worth the effort, & yet it is all so effortless. it takes greater effort not to be this. And greater effort still not to be, therefore i still am.

*　*　*

Four people died in a church fire in Ottawa 2day. i heard it on the radio, so i know it's true. it's okay though, they were believers, true Christians. they each had secret sins, i know. they didn't say that on the radio though. they never tell you the truth behind the truth.

& even as the smoke asphyxiated them, they knew there was a God & they knew that they were about to die & they knew what Hell held for them. because they were being consumed by flames. & they winked & confessed their sins & died at peace.

it's true. so easy to get to heaven after making life hell on earth for others. it's true. after making it hell. You have an out. I have an out. No matter what i've done or what you make me do, what i confess or don't confess, i have an out. What a bargoon is confession ... . what a deal what a deal what a deal ... what a deal we have in jesus, lah-de-dah-de-dah-de-dah ...

*　*　*

a woman i was having an affair with hired a private detective to find out if her husband was having an affair. the husband suspected his wife was cheating on him & he hired the same detective. i only knew this because i was having an affair with the husband too & i recommended the detective to both of them (he was a real sleaze-oid) & convinced him to tell them that neither one of them was cheating on the other & i let them live with that guilt ... but they were each so relieved that they broke off the relationship they were having with me & went back to being one happy couple who lived happily ever ... or could have ... I told you the private dick was a sleaze ball. I paid him to send them the picture that he took. She with me. He with me ... they could have lived happily ever after in their delusion, but why let them? I mean, after all, what would be the point?

*　　*　　*

My father used to trim my hair—clip clip—around my ears—clip clip—when i wanted to grow it long—clip clip—keep still, he'd say—clip clip—or i'll cut off your ear—clip, clip—but it was the sixties—clip clip—& nobody was getting clipped clipped any more so i shook my head & the son-of-a-bitch—clip clip—clipped off my ear lobe—clip clip—& he said, there, that'll teach ya—clip clip ...

But later in life, i taught him—clip clip—left him alone—clip clip—abandoned—clip clip—cut him outta my life—clip. And when his landlady called, i left him clip clip there to die like the turd he was, flushed down and away at long last flushed.

*　　*　　*

i grow old. I grow old. I shall wear my headstone cold.

*　　*　　*

Ah, goat let's me take a lunch break. Nice nanny goat ...

.

For lunch 2day, they put an apple on my tray. it looked me in the eye, winked & said:

You cannot have me, you who are tormented & tortured by a hunger for something sweet & cold & wet & intense. You who are so dry. You thirst for a bite, just a nibble. My blush tempts you tempts you, but you know to yield to temptation would be to sin again. & you have sworn never to sin again. Even so, even with your vow, you know how smooth my skin is. You hold me & caress me, looking for a bruise or blemish, a reason to devour me. But i am perfect. You have never felt skin so smooth, so unblemished. All skin you have touched has been blemished. Even yours. Especially yours. & after you have touched ... you've watched the bruises grow more intense, bruises of your own making. Never have you tasted anyone as sweet as i. Never. No one. You can only imagine how sweet my juice would taste upon your tongue, how it would bite thru the dullness of all the boring tastes you have tasted. But you cannot have me. You do not know me. You are doomed to thirst forever. To hunger for ever. To resist temptation forever more. Then & only then shall they set you free.

& i said: *Fuck you buddy!* & i ate the living day lights out of the apple. Ate it to the core. Devoured the core & spit out the seeds as i spilled my seed in my fist where the perfect apple had once been.

But it was not sweet, the eating. it was sour. the blemishes were all inside. Beneath the perfect pretence of skin unblemished, there were worms & maggots & bruised brown mush. But once having yielded to temptation, i had no choice but to devour it completely ...

i had no choice ...

Which is why they will never let me go. Will they ever let me go?

*   *   *

i thirst.

That's what my father said before i left him to die ...

She wanted me to get rid of him. She. His landlady ... she. Was. His. ... she was his m ... . she was his moth ... . she was his mother ... ...

& i ... i never knew that i had a grandmother ... and she wanted to be rid of him, but i was rid of him and was not going ... . my god, i had a grandmother and did not know it ...

what sin, what anger, what bitterness between them ... & he must've had a father ... oh my god, my father must've had a father! what sin, what anger, what bitterness must've been between them ... . i didn't know, never knew, i had a granny. And perhaps a granddaddy ...

'i thirst' is what he said before i deserted him in the desert he was lost in. in his mind. Or was it upon the cross he was. Wondered who's sins he was paying for.

The sins of his father? My father's father.

'i thirst,' he said.

'So do i,' i said. & i fled.

But for who?

Unlucky day 13 (any lucky days?)

we are in the tub, my little ZAP & i.

how old am i ...

the tub is one of those large, deep cast iron tubs with claw feet that seem as if they might rear back & dart across the bathroom floor & disappear out the door ...

we always bathed together.

he washed us.

it's saturday night. 'you gotta get clean simon if you're gonna watch the leafs play 2nite simon. she's gotta get clean before she goes to bed.'

'why can't mommy wash us?'

'get in the tub, simon. mommy is too busy washing out her sins.'

(what the fuck does he mean by that? does he know about the grocery man?)

& 2day he puts the soap in my hands & says: you're gonna do the washing ...

*   *   *

i'm healed. it worked. i'm saved. i'm fixed & well & cured. & now i wanna be free. free as the breeze in my BVDs because i have confessed & i promise i will not touch it again, my pecker, my wank, my hog, my prick, my rat, my pal, my peter, my dong. my ding-a-ling.

i mean, i've been beating, using or abusing it – or having it beaten or used or abused – every night since my first hard-on. & now i promise i will sleep thru the whole night with out ... won't jerk off to put me to sleep. won't wake up in the middle of the night & beat back my erection as it demands its share of attention. won't fuck anybody & nobody will fuck me ... i used to to do it every night, or 'twas done to me every night, & now i know i will never do it again ...

look at all i can confess to you.

i'm well, whole, cured. right?

for can't you hear me confessing for the first time, honest with myself, with the authorities—them being you, goat. & if we confess our sins & forgive our trespassers & all of that fine stuff, then you must deliver me, Goat from the evil of this place that is wearing me down & denying me all that i am & all that i ever was ...

for i shall resist temptation & i shall resist the urge to tempt anyone including myself ... i know i can do it. i can be reunited with myself & my life & maybe even my lover ...

take my rightful place in society ...

extra extra, read all about it. the pinball wizard in a miracle cure. extra!

& i owe it all to you, Goat, all to you, you tricky manipulative son of a bitch (just kidding). you're wonderful & you will be hailed by many for the miracle cure. Goat, you shall be blessed above all & given greener pastures to graze in. they'll give you the real weirdoes & sickoes & wackoes. the folks who'll make me seem like a weak cup of tea ...

if it'll help, i'll even point a few of them out so as you can get to work on them right away. Okay, Goat? i'm okay, Goat. so let me be, Goat.

but i get no answer. just a come-on from the whores on seventh avenue.

let me outta here. let me outta here. let me outta here. let me outta here. let me outta here. let me outta here ...

i don't remember any for-better-or-for-worse-til-death-do-us-part vows when i came in. nothing could be worse than putting up with you & your stinking torture for the last two fucking weeks so ...

 ... read this now. it worked. i'm an adult now. couldn't be any better. i'm healed ...

let me outta here before it gets any worse & my confessions tear me apart ...

which is why i cannot show you this, goat. Which is why i am still here. Because, there is, and i can't ...

*　　*　　*

we are in the tub, my little ZAP & i. we always bathed together. he washed us. it's saturday night. (i knew. even then i knew!)

& 2day he puts the soap in my hands & says: you're gonna do the washing ...

*　　*　　*

How can you do this to me, Goat? make me reconstruct my own videos in living nightmarish colour on the big

209

screen of my mind. & no matter how hard i try the channel zapper, i'm stuck on this arid channel without cable—i get one station & one station only. & this fucker is it. this fucker is my life. this fucker is.

It is done. I am done.

But goat said yesterday he had a surprise for me. a dénouement, so to speak. I get a day to reflect. Ha! Then, he says, I can decide. To turn this in or turn it off. All up to me. up to me. up to me, myself and Irene goodnight, Irene goodnight, goodnight ... My call. My decision…

*   *   *

So last night, i stumbled out of bed even though i was still dreaming & inhaled a cigarette even though i had quit smoking & i showered in the desert as i stepped out of the jungle & crossed the street with chickens even though there was famine in the zoo where i roamed naked even though the emperor offered me new clothes with which to cover you, sister, even though we had never met until you laughed at what it was that i forgot i had to remember even though i heard you crying at the punch line of a joke i couldn't tell even though you had heard it all before & it wasn't very funny although i never heard you say so because i was calling out your name, a name i've never mentioned, & you turned down the sheets even though i had awakened & stumbled out of bed even though you said you loved me & wrapped your naked arms around me even though they're dressed in scars i would not acknowledge even though it was my teeth that cut you even though my gums are toothless ...

*   *   *

The way things are floating up, they're gonna crucify me. but that's why i'm here, isn't it? because they tried to crucify me & failed. i fought the law and i won. i fooled them each & every one.

My punishment? This. A journal, for fuck sakes. Me, a copywriter extraordinaire, gets, by way of punishment, to keep a journal. Ha!

& even if they tried again to crucify me, i would be released if Christ would dare show his face. i would be released, exchanged for the crucifixion of an innocent man. For i am as good as Barabbas was evil.

*   *   *

Pleased to meet you, don't you know my name?

*   *   *

The Marketing Concept: You need a selected market or group of consumers, your target market, with a common need. & if you have a consumer group that has no need, you need to create a desire & then turn desire into want or need, which i excelled at. You need, of course, a product or service to fulfil the need, or ideally desire, you have created. You need to promote your product or service properly & price it appropriately. & you need to place it correctly, preferably just out of reach, so that you can watch your selected target market segment slobber like a group of crazed hyenas as it reaches for the unreachable dream ...

that was me: the marketing concept man. i sensed a need. i filled the need. I sensed no need, i created a desire. i hunted deer out of season—because there is no rhyme or reason & there is no season for hunting, dear, the way i did ...

* * *

Her butt moved like a brick wall built on a firm foundation—it wiggled not at all. That's all i remember. That & that we were really drunk. before we made love i started to sing, 'Nelly hold your belly close to mine. Wiggle your bum.'

She shushed me but she was laughing at the same time & she said that the neighbours would hear even though i could tell she didn't care. & so i wrapped my arms around her & sang some more & moved her towards the window which i opened while undressing her & i sang, 'Nelly hold your belly close to mine!'

And we made love on the window sill & her butt moved like a brick wall built on a firm foundation—it wiggled not at all.

because she had passed out.

but i kept at it until i finished even as the cats & neighbours howled out of tune with my howling ...

and when i was done, i let her go & she tumble out the window, & landed with a thud ...

one floor below.

i saw her a few evenings later, at the same bar where we had met, her arm in a sling, but i pretended that i didn't know her. Which was okay because she ignored me as i ignored her as she ignored me ...

* * *

Do you ever wonder what astronauts do in space? i mean, i know they keep busy doing astro-techno-crap & all of that. but what do they do that we don't know about?

Like, do they ever jerk off? & what would an ejaculation that defied gravity feel like, and look like? I mean, would the sperm kinda float all about until it eventually smearing their windshield? At least it wouldn't splatter all over their bellies, i don't think.

These are the questions that astronauts never get asked. Like when they're up there for months, do they give themselves extra-terrestrial blow jobs? And if there is no gravity, do they have a choice to swallow or spit? Don't they just open their mouths and watch it float up?

These things we should know, you know. i wonder if the answers, my friend, are written in an encyclopedia.

*   *   *

i sometimes think that if i could see myself, see my face—my expression—as i did things in life, i would've done things differently. you know, when i look in the mirror, the person i see is not the person who i imagine has done what I've done (allegedly, goat, allegedly) or who has had stuff done unto him. If i could see myself, if others could see themselves, would the seeing—the shock the seeing, the recognition of the doing—change the doer and the done?

maybe if i went thru life with a mirror in front of my face, i'd know who i was & why these things keep on happening to me.

Maybe.

maybe baby. but then again, maybe not.

* * *

i don't know. Maybe i'm senile. Maybe i've been senile all my life. when you lose your memory, you're senile right? i mean, i remember things. At least i think i do. i'm never really sure when i'm remembering stuff or making it up.

Do you know what that's like? Like the stuff i wrote yesterday (love was such an easy game to play). it started as a faded image etched on the naked landscape of my brain, kind of like a cave drawing, & it sort of came into focus—like a dream. (and you know how unfocused dreams can be.) i mean it could have been a dream. all of this could be a dream, as opposed to a memory. No?

who shot J. R.? nobody. it was all a dream!

i mean, if i wrote, 'And then i killed a mighty mammoth' does that mean i killed one, even if i can imagine killing one? even if i can visualize killing one? even if i draw the act of killing one on the walls of my calcified cranium?

what does anything one confesses mean? especially when one is under duress. & i am. because it is important, what happens next. If I let him, my Goat will review this shit & ask me some questions, maybe, which i may even answer & he will make his recommendation to the crown ...

'Your honour, if it please the court, my patient has been so patient. He's been a real queen. a peach. a plum.'

Do i dare? do i dare eat a peach? suck a leach? shall i be impeached for saying each to each? & a few weeks later, after eating all the mammoth meat, if i'm feeling kind of hungry & go back into the cave & see the pictures of the hunt etched upon the wall, does that mean it happened? not at all. not at all?

So who's to say whether or not the flickering images i transcribe here are true or not? what is truth? what are the consequences? i suspect only bob barker knows for sure, but they took his show off the air the air ...

sometimes, all i need is the air that i breathe ...

*   *   *

so tell me my beloved mortal what petrifies your soul?

do you really want to know about vacant-lot pages cluttered by dead-end words & chain-link rhetoric i stick my tongue to on frigid-idiot days when nothing at all is all i debate because fear of extinction means that beings frozen in time & space beneath a fine & private permafrost bellow at me bitterly, the chumps.

& if glaciated fossils presented grounds on which to repent your spontaneous imagination to save your soul from naive exuberance, would you?

yes, even as i veil my eyes before them. even as they poke & prod & mutter & nod like saints at my benediction. & would you allow such self-righteous philosophers, philanderers & philistines to stick their Pinocchio noses up your cave? & would you abide by their interpretation of dream-scape shadows on your garden wall?

in purgatory I have no choice as flickering images stretched across my calcified canvass convince me thru scrape-kneed prognosis to expiate my childhood & save my progeny from sins of the father they cannot escape.

so oblivious these dino-prophets are to their creation. as oblivious as you now chose to be.

something funny happened to me on the way to my lobotomy ... but i can't remember what it was.

as you forevermore descend within, oh rock of frigid age ...

* * *

Goat, i assure you, just as i have not killed the mighty mammoth, i have been engaged in no criminal activity. & even as i say this with conviction, i know that you will tut-tut me—which is exactly what i'm trying to tell you. There's nothing to tut-tut me about. there is no king tut-tut.

the king is dead. (tabloid news stories to the contrary, be damned.) long live rock 'n' roll!

There's nothing to regret. i didn't kill the mammoth. i didn't live in the closet. daddy never said good-night prayers with me. mummy never check franky's groceries in.

The make beleafs are not forever.

i never had a little zap sister. & if i did, we never bathed her. & if we did, it was an innocent washing. & if it was not innocent, it was not me who is guilty ... & if it is not me, then it is is is is is is is is is is daddy daddy daddy daddy who is ...

& if it is not daddy, the way things are going, they're gonna crucify me ...

*   *   *

& now all is forgotten except on the cave walls of my mind. & i'm not sure who carved my initials beneath the image that flickers still. just what the truth is, i don't know any more ... yes, i loved her. yes i loved her. oh how i loved her ... and then she said, 'Simon, I'm pregnant ... ' and i loved her no more. And ted. Is dead.

all these distorted images, blinding me—and yet never out of sight ... & i'm still hungry for mammoth meat & if you let me outta here i will not be responsible for the slaughtered deer, the slaughter, dear ...

*   *   *

such control. my pulse beats steady. my breath is steady. rock steady. for a man about to die. or tell another lie. which is worse? which comes first? which comes not at all? either? neither? am i truly senile? am i the only one? or are we a senile society? Have we lost our collective memory? Have we been reduced to scratching images on the walls & leaving the interpretation for some post-hysterical generation who will look back & say, as they shiver around the fire: The assholes killed all the woolly mammoths & left us without food or fur or flowers. only Pizza Hut & nothing but.

What i'm saying is, even if i did it (and there's no proof that i did. did what? what am i accused of?) i'm not the only one. & even if i did it, i did nothing unto others that was not done unto me.

R-E-S-P-E-C-T ... R-A-T-I-O-N-A-L-I-Z-A-T-I-O-N ... .

yeah, sure, I get it. You don't have to spell it out pour moi ...

*   *   *

& you? were you titillated when you read about it? You who put me in headlines. how does it feel? to be all alone. like a complete unknown. like a rolling stone.

Goat, my fifteen minutes are up! how old is bob dylan, anyway?

& if i'm guilty, so are you. but who are you? who who? who who? oh how i loved to rock 'n roll. how i loved to rock 'n roll them ...

& am i here so you can choose to forget that i exist? Here in the cave, in the shadows. Lurking in the back of your collective consciousness like something you remember only when you die & your life flashes before your eyes:

oh shit. We did that too, didn't we.

*   *   *

So little to write. So much time to do it. Doing it. So little to love. So much time to screw it. Screwing it.

and if god did not exist, we would create it.

well i've got news for you 2day (oh boy), it does not exist; we have made it—and we have made it in our own image: a jealous, covetous, envious, resentful, petty, ignoble, intolerant, mean, judgemental, angry, wrathful, embittered, vengeful, murderous, malevolent, vindictive, invidious, pernicious, venomous, spiteful ... it.

oh death. Now that would be a luxury. the death of us; the death of it. To expire here & now, like a patient etherized upon a table who never wakes from the operation. And all the drones will ask: Who is it? oh, it's him? Hey, are his fifteen minutes up? They're not? The corpse breathes still? Then let's us go & pay a tabloid visit.

*   *   *

i am ill. i cannot eat this lunch swill. Why do you bother, goat, to give me such breaks? This crap is uneatable.

i have perhaps a low grade flu. nobody seems to care. they say i can't go see the doctor unless it gets worse. i tell them that it is getting better all the time, but that i am worse. they do not understand. they ignore me still.

i have a headache & mild indigestion & halitosis & my ears pop when i burp as if each time i burp i'm landing back on earth from a sojourn into the stratosphere. (where the dear & the antelope play & the astronauts jerk off and blow each other in zero gravity ...) oh, the gravity of it all. Yeah, i know. Groan ... .

My tongue is dry & yellow. My headaches wax & wane like the phases of the moon. i am dying. who isn't? This is not the nausea of love, nor spring, nor war. is this something which too shall pass? As i pass gas from mouth & ass. As i too shall pass. out. away. hi-ho silver, away ...

if my friends were cactus, they would die of thirst.

*   *   *

i used to peel orange peels with a knife. try to peel one long strip. if it broke, i was told (who told me these things?) i'd have bad luck for life. My orange peels always broke.

219

For lunch, i got served an orange. Here. i'll tape the broken rind to the page for you to see & taste & smell. they serve me tea & oranges. And the dessert come all the way from a china desert ...

as delicate as fine china. as fresh as an orange fresh-picked. & she tasted like tea with a trace of honey.

*   *   *

Go away, goat. This is not why you've brought me here 2day. Not to talk about her. Leave her out of it, okay? i'll confess to anything but her. because i didn't. Nothing. i swear. i won't open my mouth, but if i could i'd swear on a stack of bibles as tall as the CN tower. Nothing happened. i didn't.

*   *   *

'Come on kids, it's time to get into the tub.'

Rub-a-dub-dub. Three in the tub ...

*   *   *

simon was a bad boy. mummy caught him with his pecker in the hole in the bedroom floor ... & mummy slapped him & strapped him.

on the table ... franky & mummy ... & where am i & where is daddy? home early?

shouts screams ... screams shouts ... tears ... prayers ... tears ... silence ... long, long, long silence ...

& i never see frankie again ... . nobody ever sees frankie again ... is that ... ? did that ... ? ever? again?

where is frankie?

*   *   *

& when ...

... was little sister born?

Little sister. I. Had. A little. Sister. But ...

she wasn't daddy's, was she?

little sister. taken like a lamb to the slaughter.

*   *   *

is this it? What you want? do you want me here?
opening doors where the rust has settled in as thick as
an ice age glacier.

but rust never sleeps, does it? And glaciers move so ...
 glacially.

Could this be thy will? because it sure as hell ain't mine.
of course the irony of this is, i don't know what i'm talking
about. Nor do you.

*   *   *

Fuck. Fuck. Fuck. The word ran thru my mind late at
night, usually on a Sunday night, like an endless loop.
Fuck Fuck. Fuck. & then i'd pray. Forgive me. Forgive
me. Forgive me. & fuck fuck fuck would come back like
an instant replay.

oh god protect me from my sin because i might die
before i awake. & then oh lord, my soul you will refuse to
take if i am thinking fuck fuck fuck ... if i should die with
fuck upon my lips, i'll burn forever & a day in hell. oh hell
fire. oh damn damnation. oh bitter fear. oh fuck upon my
lips.

oh oranges & tea with the taste of honey upon my lips.
she was so sweet ...

it's what daddy made me do ... take the lamb to slaughter.

*   *   *

The bath tub in the washroom where i sat upon the toilet, was an old enamel tub with claw feet that seemed to grip the floor. it was a large tub, large enough that when i was two or three i could sit on the edge of the tub, at the back, & slide down in to the water, splash. oh what joy to make a splash ...

daddy said: if you want to watch the make beleafs tonight, get in the tub with her simon.

monkey see. monkey do.

see no evil. hear no evil. speak no evil.

you didn't hear it. you didn't see it. you won't say nothing, never in your life ...

& 2day? but 2day? is he in the tub too? 2day he is in the tub? is he? who is in ...

& i would slide & she would laugh because she was having fun, little sister.

the taste of tea and honey upon my lips ...

if she's having fun ... then why is she crying?

2day, why is she crying?

'it's our secret, simon.'

*   *   *

'pick her up Simon. you've hurt her ... '

'but you said to ... '

*   *   *

shit no shit no shit no ...

my being here ... it has nothing to do, does it, with what happened in the tub, does it?

or pushing the drunk co-ed out the first-floor window?

or knifing her belly when she said she was pregnant?

what were they giving me the third degree for?

what crimes did they want me to confess to?

why am i hear Goat?

look how deep i am ... & still it is not deep enough.

because that is not it at all.

*   *   *

& i stepped back into the shadows. ran home to a deserted house. ET run home. hooked up cable. & ZAPped my life away ... until ... they found the illegal cable hook up & the FUCKERS cut me off ...

& later much later, they found me dancing in the park after dark by myself. it was not a lark. in the park. After dark. in the park washrooms. Sitting on the toilet. Pretending to be shitting on the toilet.

i found my thrill. on toilet park hill. The king of swill. The sultan of swing. & Harry doesn't mind if he don't make the scene. He's got a night time blow job or hand job or any other kind of job & he's doing all right ...

but that's not why i'm here.

they busted me for washroom delinquency. i served my time, two years less a day with time off for good

223

behaviour ... i was out on parole in a week ... so i served my time, paid for my so-called crime ...

* * *

'now look what you've done, simon. you've hurt her.'

'but i did what you said, daddy.'

& i became a shadow man. A mole. Living in a little hole. except he discovered my hole.

Fuck fuck. if i should die before i awake, my confession yet to make ...

why here now if not for you, little sister?

but i died long before i awoke. or at least i thought i had, until i met myself standing in the shadows. & i said to me, come home. Come home. Come home. it's supper time. it's time to be eaten alive. To sacrifice yourself on the altar of despair.

it's time, my shadow self said to me ...

& i ran back to the house, the deserted house, & i set up shop in the shadows ...

* * *

a fist full of soap. in the tub with her & a fist full of soap ...

Goat, i could be reading or eating or watching Tv even though lard-ass holds the channel zapper. but instead i choose to be here with you. aren't you flattered? what is the reward for such loyalty?

but what does it matter? when you're madder than a hatter.

time to let it all hang out, eh?

all of me hang out. all of me hanging out.

hang all of me. crucify me. free Barabbas & let me be, dear lord, let me be ...

i must be three—father son & holy spirit—inside this skin which keeps me within ... & contains my multitude of sins. the deadliest of the deadly sins. the sin with which it begins. now it begins. let it begin ... oh yes. oh yep. oh yeah. clean up time. is that what this is supposed to be.? but i'm so tired of you & you must be so tired of me.

which is why i choose to flee. Out of here, to my room ...

.

*   *   *

the cool fresh-cut grass beneath the shadow, the moon shadow of the crab apple tree, never looked so inviting.

from here i can see it under the moonlight, the mysterious moonlight, thru these bars that cross my window i can see the moon hovering above the trees casting shadows on the green grounds, shadows that spreads their arms & invite me to become one with the moon shadow moon shadow ...

and after i soil you & you soil me, i will be once again. clean up time. now it begins. begins to get better. getting better ever day in every way, better & better.

oh sure. oh yes. i believe. i do believe ...

is heaven better than this? if so, what joy & bliss.

everybody ought to go to sunday school sunday school. dressed in sunday best, clean clothes, shirt starched stiff, hiding the blackness underneath—the blackness of his heart, her heart. the blackness & blueness of my bruises ...

now it begins. but when did it begin?

clean up on saturday night, get your body clean for sunday school & sunday service where you get your soul dry cleaned for heaven, where it's very clean all the time. nobody is soiled there, they're too busy getting spoiled there ...

clean up time. we messed up little sister & now it's clean up time. oh yeah. yes. oh sure ...

*   *   *

this is my beloved dung in whom i am well displeased.

'you are my beloved,' he said.

'she is our beloved,' he said. 'and we must sacrifice our beloved in the name of our beloved lord & almighty father.'

'father forgive us for we know not what we do,' he prayed before we made our sacrifice.

*   *   *

'you are my beloved,' he said. then he nailed me to the sheets with a spear so large he ripped a hole thru me & i bled puss & blood & it burned like vinegar in my wound, it did. so badly he ripped me open in the night in the darkness in the shadows. & the neighbours found me naked on the cool fresh-cut lawn under the moonlight, under the crab apple tree. asleep in the cool fresh feel of the earth.

& they called my parents who took me home & bathed me & the next day dressed me in my clean, starched sunday best & took me to sunday school sunday school everybody ought to go to sunday school & my father made me confess my sins: the sins of the father ...

*   *   *

called her, he did, his fallen angel, is what he called her.

& i was his silent angel. & you ask why i don't talk now? you know why? i am my father. & i am sworn to silence. because if you don't say it you haven't done it; if you don't think it, it is not so. & these pages, Goat, that i write ... you will never read them. trust me on that. as loud as these pages get, they don't get loud enough to be read.

if a confession falls in a forest & there is nobody there to hear it, then is it a confession?

these pages, Goat, will burn in hell with me.

*   *   *

garbage goes out 2morrow. i know the schedule. garbage out 2morrow ... i know where the big bins are & 2morrow it's garbage out. 2morrow these pages & i go ... out out damn spot ... we go out & we get incinerated. we go out & go to hell, Goat. that's where you go if you stop going to sunday school. fuck fuck fuck upon my lips like the taste of tea & honey ... & tomorrow i go to hell to burn forever more ... to hell to burn forever more.

& even if you were to set me free, you could never set me free. don't you see? don't you see? you could never set me free from the hell i am. from the hell that awaits me ...

227

and thinking it over, i've been sad. & thinking it over i'd be more than glad to change my ways. but nobody ever asked me to.

ah, but mine was actually a joyous boyhood. right? oh what a life i had. what a lovely lovely life i had ...

that is why, in the museum program publicizing an exhibit of fossils that once had been my childhood there is a black & white photograph of me—the only one remaining from the 4-for-a-quarter pictures i took in the curtained booth at the shopping mall the first time i swiped money from my mother's purse. this child, the archaeologist's write-up accompanying the photograph asserts, was alive during the plasticine period (although it is doubtful anybody noticed) & he is presumed to have died shortly after completing the finger-paintings his mother refused to tape to the fridge. several insignificant fragments were preserved amongst the dust balls that accumulated under the bed he wet almost every night.

the exhibit also includes my report cards complete with D's, E's & F's & teacher's comments: - refuses to participate ... - contributes nothing to class ... - is listless & bored ... - disrupts others ... - picks his nose ... - smells of urine ... - enjoys finger-painting ...

& visitors may listen to time-warped tapes of old friends chanting: - stepped on a crack you broke your mother's back ... - fatso is stupid fatso is stupid ... - liar liar pants on fire got hung up on the telephone wires ... - you looked you looked you dirty crook you stole your mother's pocket book (how did they know?)

the brochure also describes how my frail skull was found buried in the playground sand pit where i hid to escaped schoolmates ranting about gold stars & straight A's ...

petrified, he stuck it out in his new habitat until his fossilized remains were exhumed for exhibit in this hermetically-sealed display case illuminated by ...

... life flashes before my eyes ...

& if i had not already died, i would scream & scream the primal scream of victim earth—the agony of history about to repeat itself (yet again) as mothers gawk & fathers yawn before what remains ... & they do not see how kaleidoscopic the finger-paintings were:

*   *   *

& so here & now & it all comes floating up ... & just what the fuck am i supposed to do with images of somebody else's rotten memories that obliterate all that i was, my happy childhood?

oh happy days. When the sun did shine. instead of this: confined to darkness except for the light cast by the flickering flames of hell ... in the hell that other people have made for me. Forevermore to burn ...

And in the End DAY 14!

Woke up. Got out of bed. Dragged a comb across my head. There was no bus to catch. i had so many seconds left. So i continued on this journey instead ...

Two weeks, goat promised me. two weeks. 7 days makes one weak, but 14 days = 2 weeks. I'm all but done and outta here, y'all! When do we get this over with, goat?

*　*　*

why bother relating my dreams. i mean, did i even sleep last night? last night, i didn't get to sleep at all ...　Goat, i am doing your job here, & not getting paid for it ...　or am i paying for it ...

i surrender all. all to Goat now i surrender. i surrender all.

in church one day, i had a vision. god smiled upon me. & i made a decision. i decide to break my vow of silence even if it was an unpardonable sin to break a vow made to your father before god, made to your father who you were supposed to honour as you would god, who you were to absolutely honour at the risk of eternal damnation.

yes. break my vow. tell the preacher man what had gone down, and who had gone done on whom ...

after the service i went to see him. after each service he went into a room behind the auditorium—his personal prayer room—and met people in need.

i swear i knocked. lightly no doubt. hell, i was scared. even so, i swear i knocked.

i did not barge in like he accused me of doing.

what does it matter what i did. somebody in need got there before me to confess all to him. at least that's what i figured she was doing, on her knees before the preacher who sat in his leather chair, low moans emanating from a half-smile on his pudgy red face.

mr. pig-face, we called him.

she got there before me to surrender all to the preacher, who was surrendering all that she cook take from him, on her knees before him ...

while daddy chortled with his cronies after the service & went to the restaurant with them to drink coffee & to discuss the make beleafs forever, she surrendered all.

& i swear i knocked.

& the preacher condemned me & damned me to eternal hell fire & brimstone—his face as red as a devil as he raged hell fire & brimstone upon me.

& she buttoned her blouse & straightened her dress, her sunday best dress, & took my hand & took me out to the car to wait for my father who art in restaurant: her husband ...

*   *   *

now i had two vows of silence to keep. one to daddy & one to mummy.

*   *   *

how old was i? 8, 9, 10?

that's how old i feel i was. some days that's how old i feel i am still. i was so much younger then. i'm older than that now.

my feet are cold. my feet are cold. i should remove these paper slippers & slip on warmer thoughts ...

you surrendered all little sister. we took all you had from you.

* * *

fish bowl is what i lived in with both of them waiting to pounce upon me the moment they suspected i was my vow was weakening. Neither knowing what the other knew.

& i proved over & over & over again that they could trust me even as they had betrayed my trust, only i didn't know it could get any worse: my childhood.

but it got worse because they could not trust themselves.

* * *

'we were just about to pray,' mummy said to me as we sat in the car and waited for pa: Pig-face & i.' (only she didn't call him pig-face. & neither dis i, at least not to her face.) '& you barged in.'

'i knocked.'

'shut-up. you barged in & saw us praying & now you know my sins are forgiven. & you will not say a word to anybody or you will rot in hell forever. & then you'll never go to heaven. & you'll never see your sister again.'

& so when she asked me what i saw, i said, 'i saw you & the pastor praying.'

*   *   *

i LOVE YOU, little sister. i know how you got to heaven, only i'm not supposed to tell. i promised. but i can write it, Goat. right? isn't that what this time has been about?

i LOVE YOU!

words my father never spoke to me.

words my mother never spoke to me.

words i never spoke to my lover.

words i never told my sister.

& so i spent my childhood in silence & kept my eyes forward so i would not see anything again except the Tv screen i before me ...

it was before you were born, little sister, that daddy & mummy fought worse than they ever fought before ... & the grocery boy stopped delivering the groceries ...

& then came you ...

& then you were gone. baptised in the bathtub. How old were you, then? How old would you now be?

'we're gonna play rub-a-dub-dub and all get baptised in the tub,' is what daddy said. it was not the first time we played that game, was it little sister? but 2nite was the last time.

under you went, my head held between you legs; your head held under the water ...

& when he let go of my head, i surfaced with the taste of tea & honey on my lips, but you ... you never floated back up to the surface, did you little sister?

233

how did he get away with it? he served no time for his crime.

this is how he got away with it:

he left us alone after it was done. he told me not to leave the tub. i watched your pale face, partially submerged still, as it turn blue ... but i did not leave the tub ...

& when he came back in ... he screamed

OH! MY! GOD!

an accident ... that is how he got away with it.

the authorities. ruled her death an accident. oh, he was found negligent of something-or-other & got his wrists slapped. but the judge saw his remorse & said his guilt was punishment enough.

& mummy? she hardly talked any more to him or me. not that she talked a lot before. But she went a lot to the preacher's private prayer room after sunday morning services.

i swear i knocked.

i swear i didn't hold her head under.

i swear he said: 'she's gonna like this simon.'

& he left me in the tub, the white iron tub with claw feet ... it was so much fun ... you could slide down the back of the tub into the water ...

he left me alone with ... her face turning blue ...

& except for one brief season when i thought i'd become someone other than who i am, i spent most of my days & most of my nights watching Tv—all day & all night except when i went out to roam the streets & get into whatever shit it was that i got into ...

things like ... going back to see mr. minister how many years later—& this time i didn't knock. no. i just burst in & caught him alone, in prayer. on his knees. He had sooooo much to repent for ... that's how i caught him when i wrapped the cord i brought with me around his neck. & i pulled tight until he did what i told him to do: 'drop ye your baggy drawers, hallelujah. spread ye your pimply cheeks, hallelujah ... ' & i banged away ... until hallelujah ... & i left him lying there, bent over in prayer ...

*   *   *

oh little sister.

*   *   *

Everybody ought to go to Sunday school. Sunday school. Sunday school. Everybody aught to learn the golden rule. Golden rule. Golden rule. Do unto others as they did on to you ...

*   *   *

On the street where i grew up. in the tub where i threw up. Daddy said, 'it's okay' as we played yellow (we played yellow) submarine (submarine). Sink the ship with torpedo. that's what captain made me do ...

he had his way with us. We were not to fuss. What more do you want. He did it. All of it. & for his sins, he died alone, on a couch in his mother's house, and she preferred that he be anywhere but there. But i sure as hell wasn't taking him home with me. although i felt ...

(no i didn't, not a bit of pity. no pity for the wicked no!) & then, when i got home, my lover (oh my love!) said she was pregnant ... What did you expect me to do? Hang around to do unto others as had been done onto me?

So i split. into to two. Maybe more. i regressed. 2nd childhood. Only i was doing the doing. Not having the doings done unto me ... simple as that. That simple.

So there, Goat, what to do with my confession? Why not rescue me from this slow passage of my life before mine eyes have seen the glory of the coming of the ...

is this a real life? or is it just fantasy? Easy come easy go. They will not let me go, these memories. Or are they just fantasies.

Goat, i'm drowning and you're not here to save me ... i'd like to call for help but i can't speak under water. and if i stay under for too long, i too may never float up ...

Tommy can you hear me? Too many wicked Uncle Ernies i have known. & grown up to be one, worse than all the other ones. No, say it ain't so. Tell me i did none of what i've written—and none of what i have not written. tell me it ain't so.

Why can't i speak, Goat. Who's got my tongue? Oh tongues of fire anoint my head & burn my brow ...

it's going to hurt, he said, when you pray because tongues of fire are going to burn the devil out of you he said when you pray. i didn't know he was hurting me. i thought it was the devil behind me, being burned the hell out of me. 'get thee behind me satan,' he said in a low moan, and he had me from behind, did satan.

236

*   *   *

fuck fuck fuck fuck ... the words invade my head against my will. i could not help but sin. i could not help it when i prayed & the good lord burnt the devil out of me ...

i am a man more sinned against than sinning. Sons of bitches pull down your britches. Here comes the flogging. Right where it itches ...

*   *   *

At football games we chanted: 'Rah rah ree. Kick him in the knee. Rah rah ruts. Kick him in the other knee.' Once at a football game as i chanted, a gaggle of girls from the opposition school came by, heading to their seats on the far side of the stadium.

'Rah rah rec. Kick him in the knee.'

One of them looked at me & smiled.

'Rah rah ruts.'

Like a fool i smiled back. Hell, we were only on opposites sides of football teams. We weren't at war.

She kneed me in the nuts.

i collapsed. My comrades laughed. Go get her, man, they said. Go get her. But i was writhing on the ground, in pain—searing burning pain. i couldn't get up, let alone get her. & after that, my friends called me mr. pussy-whipped.

*   *   *

& if i give you this, Goat, i'll never get the fuck out of here. will i? But you've known that all along, eh? That's what they pay you for. & if i don't give it you, you'll tell

237

them that i am mad (he doesn't know about himself what i know about him) & i'll never get the fuck out of here anyway.

Anyway you look at it, i lose, Mrs. Robinson.

*　　*　　*

Yes there was a woman that i loved. For a night. During foreplay, her nipples got as hard as pebbles. i bit on them until they bled. She did not whimper. in fact she moaned for me. And she charged me extra for the evening. but this is not criminal, you say. OK, technically it is, but just about every guy is doing it, so this is just me showing you that i am human too.

*　　*　　*

Suicide is a state of being you outgrow, unless of course you succeed. That's why i'm still here, Goat. i failed miserably at it.

*　　*　　*

My life: A peanut sat on the rail road track, his heart was all a flutter. A train came racing down the track: toot-toot. Peanut butter.

*　　*　　*

Don't touch that dial, we'll be back after a word from our father which art in heaven hallowed be thy name game, banana-rama fee-fi po-pana, fee fi fo fum i smell the blood of the lamb who's fleece was white as snow so when it went baa-baa-baa thru harlem, it got mugged by black sheep black sheep have you any wool, yes sir, yes sir, three bags full of shit like this ...

*　　*　　*

puff the channel changer lived by Tv & frolicked in the phosphorous glow of living colour fantasy ... big G, little o, gives you go fuck yourself ... cans or drafts or bottles it's our favourite brew. we'll drink carling red crap, we are drinkers true ... the one an only cereal that comes in the shape of animals ... The lord is my shepherd, i shall not be wanton ...

*   *   *

i'd like to describe the closet where i hid for what feels like forever, but is was so dark. i'm in there, still. so still i was in there. it did smell, come to think of it, of wet wool—mittens & scarves, boots & socks. it smelled like a barn, in the closet where i grew up.

What was i doing there? Nobody else was there is what i was doing there. I was being alone is what i was doing there. i was enjoying the darkness is what i was doing there. i was sniffing mittens & scarves & boots & socks.

My secret place. That's what i called it. Gonna take you to my secret place ...

& sometimes i'd be in my place & the door would open & the hall light would illuminate the darkness. & i'd scrunch myself into an invisible ball in one corner pocket of the closet & he would put on his coat & i'd stay scrunched in the corner until he slammed the door & darkness settled over me again ...

it feels like a lifetime i spent in that closet. yet it was only one season: winter. The winter after the bath. because by the summer father left mother for a long, what seemed like and endless, season. until the call that said he was dying & i came to see him die.

and mother & i?

am i heading for the light?

if i'm still in hiding, does it means he hasn't found me. is that what it means? is it? What is it? What is it? Let us go & pay a visit. Haven't a clue what you do, daddy when you put your coat on & wrap your scarf around your neck. Where do you go? What do you do? Who do you do it to?

Not to me any more. 'Cause you can't find me any more. 'Cause i'm never coming into the light again ...

but what about mummy?

*   *   *

it was not all that long ago, it seems, that i threw out my Tv set & vcr because i got up one day & realized that they were evil. of the devil. the devil had me addicted to them. me & my penis. i was worshipping false idols. at least false boobs & cunts & fornication.

to think, i started with romper room ... then moved on to the harder stuff ... until eventually the snuff stuff ...

*   *   *

mother & i stayed together.

*   *   *

& god tried to punish me for watching too much Tv. it punished me & with each punishment, i'd pay for my sins, ask forgiveness & quit—for a season.

it almost burned out my eyes one night using the iron— but only managed to burn my cheek. it busted my fingers

240

one night in the vice so i couldn't operate the channel changer.

how often did i reform? ask for forgiveness & strength. to no avail. like an alcoholic constantly falling off the wagon. you should see my bruises.

belly bruises, in places where you're least likely to see them: that's what father gave mother. belly bruises. he slowly slit her emotional jugular & nobody noticed.

but you got yours, didn't you ma? you got me, didn't you ma?

pa knew there was a way to get to you. the grocery delivery boy's daughter ... like a lamb, led to the slaughter ...

& he used me to hurt her to get to you. & that was no belly bruise. i could see the hurt carved across your face, so intense, as if we had raped you with a dull razor.

the dull razor i took to my wrists how many years later while watching a snuff movie in which some guy ... his little sister ... & by the time i got out off the hospital, all was as if all was forgotten again. Verging on pleasant. & i almost thought i could live that life forever ...

but then oh Goat oh no oh Goat oh no ... proof shit floats ... i am proof shit floats ... i am ivory snow ... 99-1/4% pure ... & i am shit ... i float ...

after she said ... having your baby and i do it to her ... and run. & i am home—the deserted house where i grew up ... this is how it's supposed to be: i am at long last in control, truly alone and in control. & i get me a

brand new coloured Tv & hook up the cable illegally ...
could heaven be better than this?

Until ... what are those workers doing out there, in front
of my house? unhooking the cable Tv ... the assholes ...
float shit float ... & so home alone without even the
company of Tv i am & i wandered the streets &
discovered many who had no home ... so many of them.
& i said: we are family. & they became my sons &
daughters. amazing (grace) what a good washing & a bit
of food can do for a ragged street urchin. yes, how i
loved to care for my little boys & girls who were looking
for a father ... my bad little boys & girls who could make
their father who art not in heaven oh so mad. & i had to,
you know, punish them & make them pray for
forgiveness ... because sometimes they had made their
father who art not ... mad! Mad, i say, mad, mad, mad ...

and when i tired of them, i changed them—ZAP—no
problem.

I was expecting something here. The burden, like the
stone that entombed Him, rolled away. But it sits there
still, no rolling away. No relief. Imprisoned still ... and
here I thought confession was good for the soul. Ha!

*   *   *

that's what he told me. that little sister had been bad &
that she had made him mad. & we had to baptise her
and free her from evil.

i had to mummy 'cause daddy said i had to & i had to
show daddy that i was his beloved son in whom he
would not be well pleased if i didn't. & so i had to ...

242

just like i had to do what i had to do to the bad little girls & the bad little boys ...

help, i need somebody. not just anybody. oh won't you please please me like i do when i please you ...

the body is a borderline. it separates what we feel inside from what we feel outside. and inside i feel an emotional void. nothing. emptiness. less than nothing. chaos. in the beginning.

but what i want to feel is regret & pain & remorse. what i want is to feel. i want to suffer for my sins. i would volunteer to go to any torture state, to let them test their latest torture methods on me, if i thought it would make me feel ...

but what they would do to me would be on the edge of the border line. they would do it to my body ... how do i get inside? how do i get my mind to feel what my body feels as it is stretched out on the rack full of nails, nails that impale my every pore ... how to get to my mind, to get me to mind?

but no, there is no crossing the borderline. my mind is independent of my body & has always been. or i would not be here 2day—would not have survived ...

... survived beyond the grocery boy dressing me in my mother's clothes & ...

... survived beyond whatever day it was when i saw mummy on the table ...

. ... survived beyond every night my father knelt behind me to help me say my get-thee-behind-me satan prayers ...

... survived beyond little sister ...

... survived beyond the sunday when i saw mummy praying with the preacher ...

... survived beyond Ted who is dead ...

... survived beyond the cutting her when she said she was ...

... survived beyond turning my back on father as he lay dying ...

... survived beyond forever and a day this feels like ...

that's me, Goat, isn't it: a survivor ... I will survive. You sing it sister ... Creating so many other survivors ... That's me. More fodder for goat food I bring to you.

the only good thing i did in my life, you know, was run away that day. but look at all since. has my mind had anything to do with it? i think not. i don't know. but if i think not, therefore i am not. No? i don't know. i do not know. oh my naked body. my naked mind. does it matter who is to blame for the pain the pain the pain ... that will not cross the boarder line ...

*   *   *

if i had known that eating of this fruit would make me ashamed ...

the snake! it made me do it ...

i am naked lord & so ashamed. can you forgive me or will you cast me out of this ... this what? this is not my beautiful house. this is not my beautiful wife. this is not the life i wanted or asked for or chose.

i had no choice, Goat. my mind tried its best to protect my body. it did what it could do. it was not enough. my body did not reciprocate. it did nothing to protect my mind.

I was just following orders ... ah, but we know where that line of defence gets you. Sins of the father sins of the father sins of the father ... those were my marching orders, goat. Ah, but we know where the defence of just following orders gets you, goat. straight into the belly of hell. Which, if you want a true confession, i confess is where i deserve to be. I do. I confess. I confess it all. (all to besus, I confess it...) In fact, i'll pull the leaver that opens the trap door through which i'll fall and husha husha i will fall down, straight to hell, with pleasure, goat. I just need a little help from my friends to get there. Where is the door? Where is the lever? Tell me tell me tell me. i need a little help because i am a coward and try as i might, i have not had the courage to send myself to hell.

will you try to rescue me from this closet in which i have hidden myself forever? will you try Goat? Me thinks i'd rather you show me the lever.

there's the rub. the back rub. ah the back rub i could give you Goat ...

so can i trust you Goat, to rescue me? because it is anathema to your reason for being to show me the leaver, so i trust you, goat, because trusting you is my ticket outta here. isn't it Goat? tell me i'm gonna get out of here. this isn't a life sentence, Goat. i may be insane, but i am not guilty!

except if i trust you Goat, i might discover ... discover
what? discover that i have not spent my entire life in hell.
no, that is not it at all ... i might discover that i ... am ...
hell ...

And why no goat before me now?

Fuck, yet another DAY

2 weeks is 14 days, but he did not call me in, goat did not, at end of yesterday, all my troubles seemed so far away ... love is a fucking difficult game to play, unless your hard and then it's like hey and anyway ...

It's done... 14 days plus this one. Th'orderly says goat wants soon to see me today. So it's done. I can quit this now, or soon, by end of day. At the end of the day, it shall be finished, I shall be done, I shall be released.

My pursuit of the character Me a name I call myself is done.

Once I am before goat... I shall be ... until them, let me make a note, or two, or three... but soon, I shall hear from goat, and all this shall be done. This too shall pass. It shall be finished.

*　　*　　*

where have all the goat dreams gone? long time passing. where have all the goat dreams gone, just f-f-faded away ... is this significant, goat? i know that i dreamt last night—but i can't remember what i dreamt about ... i can make one up for you, if you're interested.

let's see ... last night i dreamt of playing Frisbee by myself in the back yard of the house where i grew up in a rain storm & i missed every toss until the skies cleared & only a rainbow remained & i caught one & to celebrate, i made one last toss... so high high high in the sky i threw the Frisbee that it ruptured heaven & it was suddenly midnight & down down down she tumbled, a pretty blonde star ... & i held out my arms for her & yes! yes! yes! i ... caught her & swore that i would never ever let her go ...

* * *

round ball round ball pull the baby's hair & cut it & cut it & cut it & cut it & tickle under there ... he – he – he... he used to do that tickle under there, to little sister ... he used to play round ball with her ... *round ball round ball pull the baby's hair* – the parent is supposed to tug gently on a lock of hair & put it in the child's hand. & *cut it & cut it & cut it & cut it* – & pretend to cut it & cut it. & *tickle under there* – & then tickle her gently under the arm pits & make the child laugh ... LAUGH, Goat! Laugh. not CRY!

he pulled out locks of her golden blonde hair. he laid the hair in her hand & he sliced it and sliced it and sliced it ... with a razor blade... & made her bleed. & then he wiped her blood on his hand & and & and ... Tickled UNDER... under... there...

& you know Goat, when she died, he got thee behind me, my satan did, & we said our prayers together ... under there...

so what was i supposed to do?

Go ahead, feel sorry for me. because i cannot feel sorry for myself ... or do not. It simply does not matter what you feel. Nor, any longer, that I feel. Never have and never will.

Am I sorry for what became of me? of what the me I became perpetuated?

Does it matter? Will it help if I say yes? Who will it help? There are those who needed help, and it will not help – not at all. Will not cannot. So what's the point in feeling or saying what I feel? What be the point?

'Eat your vegetables,' mama would say. 'There are children starving in india.' (or was it China?) (does it matter where they are starving?) So i ate my vegetables. But the children continued to starve. So i ate more vegetables & i ate everything else mama put on my plate. in fact, i begged for seconds & sometimes thirds. & mama was pleased & proud. But still the children starved. & starved. No matter how much I ate, it mattered not. Even as i became a tub of lard, the children starved. It matters not.

so?

is there hope for this dope? or is there just money for rope?

i am. & she is. & she was. & we are. & we were. but we're not. any more. which is why. feel this way. & her? did i ever? of course, we must consider. & then there are. but we want. at least i. & does she? do i? if not, what? & even then, then what? this? this is not. even if we are & were, but we're not—any more. so there. & more often than not. but not very. in fact, hardly. ever. ever? & yet, now? yet now. yes now. oh never. mind. & am i? & is she? & were we? ever? ever again?

i am thinking of something even as i write. in other words, i am not thinking about what i am writing nor am i writing about what i am thinking.

Oh, why not spit it out? why not shout it out? why not spill it out? why not dump it out like a bucket of vomit? why keep troubled waters still?

this is the thought:

all that i've said about all that i've done & about all that's been done ... so what?

i am me & you are you & i am here & i am going nowhere. & the victimizers are still victimizing & the victims are still being victimized. old black joe is still picking cotton. & i am still stinkin' rotten. to the core, goat. to the core. even a worm, goat, would find no flesh on this core. even the worms, goat, have vacated this bit of rotted-to-the-core.

& even so, so what? so what do we do with it goat? what do i do with it?

perhaps you care how this all turns out? perhaps. perhaps though you just work at your job, collect your pay. & you don't give a fuck if i go slip sliding away up the river for a lifetime of drowning in whatever it is that floats to the surface & holds me under forever ...

i mean, why would he care? why should he care? if he cared he would've interfere with this hell i am putting myself thru to please him. he would've interceded if he cared. & even if he cared, where would his caring get me?

*   *   *

he put the soap in my hands & said, 2day you're gonna do the rub-a-dub-dub. & he made me wash her clean, in the tub, my daddy did, because he said she was dirty

dirty dirty. he said she was as dirty as mummy. & then he let the water out of the tub & said: there. all her dirty has gone down the drain. gone down the drain to hell.

& we were naked in the tub & it was cold in the tub. & she shivered & i shivered & daddy laughed.

he makes me put my hands in her places & my tongue in her places & i get ... excited. do you know how old i am? how old i really am? & how old she is? i am old enough to know this is wrong, goat.

old enough to get excited & hard ...

& i get hard & he laughs & says, good good. as good as daddy. good good. you're a man my son. my beloved son in whom i am well pleased. a man like daddy.

& he shows me where to put my hardness amongst the garbage & the flowers.

he says she is garbage & you are going to take her flower.

& he makes me put my hardness in her soft, flower place. & he laughs & he says good good you're a man my son a man my beloved son.

& she cries. she cries. & i love her but i don't care that she cries because ... i don't care that anybody is crying because i am ... even though i don't know what it is that I am doing and what is happening, and even though what is happening feels soooo good and soothing and so fine… & daddy is laughing, good good, & i am laughing, good good. & she is crying.

she's no good, daddy says. you're so good, daddy says.

& is that mamma pounding at the door, screaming behind the door?

mamma screaming. sister crying. simon coming lord, coming home to you ...

& he filled up the tub & held her head under until ...

& he told the coroner that he had left the room and when he returned ... I heard him return and scream: DROWNED! MY BABY! DROWNED!

And mommy is where?

*   *   *

jesus loves me this i know ... red & yellow black & white they are precious in his sight (HA!). he sees the little sparrow fall and does not catch her, NO. DOES NOT CATCH HER NOT AT ALL!

*   *   *

this is my lifeline, is it not? is that not what this has become? did you know what it would become? this has nothing to do with sanity or insanity, with guilty or not guilty.

it has everything to do with my internal freedom & nothing to do with my external freedom. for i have been a prisoner for a long, long time. & even though the authorities will never set me free, soon i will set me free.

i am not going free. did i ever go free?

to stop is to write: *it is finished* & to say no more.

nudge-nudge. wink-wink. say no more.

aren't you proud of me? i still have my sense of humour intact. ha ha ha.

i cannot stop ... i cannot write *it is finished* here because ... it is not finished. is it?

no.

i would like to say no more say no more but there are things to be said before i sleep forever more. forever more. there are miles to go before i sleep forever more ...

there is this to be said, before i lay me down to sleep forever more:

i am done, & now daddy is running water into the tub.

for the baptismal, is what he says.

now we must baptise her & save her soul ...

crying. pounding. screaming. water running. sister drowning ... just when you think it is finished ...

& now i am not in the tub. i am sitting on the toilet beside the tub. but where is daddy?

he is in ... as the tub fills again ... he has her too. he has her too. oh god he has her too ...

daddy never left the room ...

when mummy broke thru the door, this is what she saw:

sister no longer crying. the water over her head.

daddy grunting. still doing it to her.

sister is dead.

me on the toilet... but where is ted?

& I heard the hellish scream that ripped mother asunder.

But daddy said he left the room ...

'a sad but simple case of drowning,' said the coroner, and the judge and jury agreed.

why mother? whey did you remain silent?

about little sister, i never did cry. even now, you think i should cry. you think i should feel it across the borderline, inside, where it should hurt & i should burn like hell. you would think, wouldn't you? you would think ...

this is it then, goat. All the other stuff, yes. But this is at the rotten core of it all.

& even though capital punishment has been outlawed, i am allowed to take my own life, with these words—the weapons you have given me, goat. my pen a sword to use against mine enemies. but i have no enemies, save me ...

these words... even though i have not spoken a word. inside, i have screamed my sister's tears all my life, I have screamed mother's scream all my life.

& i have searched in vain—thru Tv channels, sex in the shadows, love (ha!) & betrayal. walking away all my life, from ted and her with her belly filling up with my progeny, from my daddy's death & even my return home ... i have searched for ways to silence their screams. & now i have succeeded, here, to silence the screams. And now, that it is all at long last silent inside...

i hate honesty.

cruel & inhumane punishment, that is what the supreme court would find this treatment, goat. but what of the court that reigns Supreme. bah. a figment of some biblical copywriter's fertile imagination.

*   *   *

one cool spring evening they found me. curled up on the fresh-cut front lawn beneath a lilac tree. that was the first evening, as far as i can remember, that daddy & i prayed together. how i love the smell of fresh-cut grass. how i love to sleep on lawns, fresh cut lawns, in the evening. how i love to feel the coolness of the grass, smell the fragrance of the grass. feel the touch of grass & earth, the cool damp grass & earth.

if that is where i go when i die, where it is damp & cool, then i will enjoy my death ...

if if if if if if if ...

rough hands found me. rough hands & an official voice woke me. they woke me, they did. 'Come child,' the voice said. & the hands lifted me off the cool dampness into which i had rolled myself. they woke me from a most beautiful dream. a dream that i cannot recall. only the feeling—cool & damp & free, like flying thru mist. maybe that's what i was dreaming, that i was flying thru mist. escaping & hoping that i would never be missed ... & i cried, not because they found me, but because they woke me & i lost the feeling—the cool damp feeling of freedom.

*   *   *

Goat, i need to know, what kind of head game is it that you're playing with me? the worst kind i imagine. you give me blood, you give me pen. you say spill your blood upon the page & confess. & when i confess, i discover still that there is still no hope.

head games, goat, more vicious than any head i could ever demand, or give.

* * *

i have a plan. i will walk into goat's office now & tell him (yes break my vow of silence & shout it out at him):

i'm healed. it worked. i'm saved. i'm fixed & well & cured. & now i wanna be free.

* * *

shit, i shouldn't've done it. i mean all i wanted was for him to read it, my confession. for him to hear it, my confession. for him to see exactly how he had broken me, house trained me. that's all i wanted to tell him, or to have him read. how well i was doing.

so that he could give me his diagnosis & then his prognosis.

I'm not sure why I wasn't in goat's office today, my last day … not sure why I was in my room, door locked … which is why, to get to goat, to show him this is my life, I had to call the orderly and, of course, i had to take out the orderly to get outta here …

& then, down the hall, lard-ass, the son-of-a-bitch, was coming outta of the washroom where he had, no doubt, taken another lard-ass crap & not wiped his ass. he had to go down too. a boot to the balls (even with these paper slippers i can still kick with the best of them) & he went down like a ton of bricks built on a sand foundation during an earthquake.

& i had to knock over the receptionist who tried to keep me out of goat's office. i mean, how else was he gonna know how happy he had made me. & there the fuck he was, with ... another patient ...

it was bad enough that the two-timing goat was with another ... i thought he was devoting his undivided attention to me—just waiting & anticipating the moment that i came to surrender all to him ... but what was worse, was that goat was not talking & the patient was not talking. no. goat was sitting in his chair, his back to me ...

the patient was on his knees ... before him, in prayer ... just like mummy & the minister ...

*   *   *

is that what i saw? i don't remember what i saw at all at all. all i know is what i saw flicker in the big screen behind my eyes.

goat was with another. & bang bang maxwell's silver hammer came down upon their heads. I know were maxwell keeps his silver hammer ... then goat opened his billy-goat gruff mouth & strange words—words that i had heard before—words for which he would have to ask forgiveness, spilled forth from his mouth:

fuck fuck fuck fuck fuck fuck fuck ...

& i knew then that he had not yet died on the cross for my redemption & i knew then that it was time to crucify him—to nail him to the cross with my flailing fists & bang his head against the wall until it bled ...

& then i flew down the hall & out the door marked emergency. & i flew into the snow & the sleet. & i was free. free to fly as far away as i could fly.

*   *   *

but i did not fly far at all. the authorities found me naked, rolled into a ball in the snow, beneath a stripped naked lilac tree ... i guess i didn't know that i couldn't fly at all— that my wings had long ago been clipped ...

*   *   *

but goat must still love me because he made them return this to me, the pages all intact.

so i could carry on ...

yes, he lets me carry on to make it up to him. i know i have to make it up to him. i know he'll understand. that i grew impatient for somebody to witness this, my confession. & to promise me my release for such good behaviour ... because this is a step forward—a sure-footed step towards freedom ...

goat understands. this is a reprieve. he understands that what floats to the surface can disturb the surface. he knows that soon i will talk. he knows that i am doing good work here—that the surface got rough & i sank, temporarily, beneath the white-capped waves. he knows that soon i will talk. that soon i will take his hand & walk across the surface of the stormy sea ... there is hope yet.

*   *   *

… they let me go. they didn't give a damn about what i had done to her—that i had cut her. she wouldn't testify & so they let me go free.

oh, they took my fingerprints & tried to scare the shit outta me. but then they let me go. & i ran and ran & found myself back home. & for the first time in my life … i wept.

i wept because they had let me go free & i knew i didn't deserve to be free.

just like they had let daddy go free ... & he too ran home to his mummy. only when i ran home, mother was gone. the house was abandoned & boarded up.

it was the perfect house.

*   *   *

Stalking deer out of season, is what i did. For there is no season for what i did.

*   *   *

it's snowing again. Will my life ever end?

Winter was the season that i hated it, that January weather. Relentless. That's what i hated about it. Day after day of snow and cold and cold and snow ...

And everybody bundled up. Shapeless. Nothing to get excited about. Nothing to keep me warm.

But then, here comes the sun. Little darling, its been a long, long cold winter. Here comes the sun. All right! And the wraps would peel off under the glare of the sun. And fun fun fun, until mummy let my daddy go away ...

*   *   *

but i knew all along, didn't i, that mother wouldn't be there—i knew mother had set herself free.

i knew all of this because i pulled her fucking head out of the fucking oven. And I know where Maxwell's silver hammer is ...

& i decided that if they ever caught me again, i'd make sure there was no reason for them to let me go.

do you hear me goat? do you know what i mean?

do you really want to read this? do i really have to write it ... the reason i can never go free?

* * *

damn it, make me talk ...

break me down, goat. you can do it. i don't want to go anywhere. i don't even want to go home. i want to be heard. they never listened to my screams, goat. because i couldn't get them out. i couldn't articulate the screams that tore my insides apart.

who are *they*? anyfuckingbody!

damn it. damn you. damn it all.

* * *

confession? is that what this is all about? good for the soul? have i a soul? if i do, it's damned. damned to hell. & hell i suspect is a much finer place than this. hell's a fine & private place where no one there dares embrace ...

* * *

so i moved into the abandoned house, the one with the rusted-out '54 chevy parked on blocks in the driveway, as if somebody was hoping to revive it one day. Ha.

squatters' rights, i figured. & then i made my masterpiece. the two thieves on Calvary would've felt right at home on the crosses i constructed in the basement.

crosses. yes. christ was cross. he was hammered. . I know were maxwell keeps his silver hammer … nailed to the cross. if it be thy will. & his father said, hang in there my beloved.

& yet, my god, christ said forgive them for they know not what they do. the fool. he said that. i read that. i built my crosses & i knew what it was i had to do—& i knew that he would forgive me. the fool. because it is written: father forgive them for they know not what they do.

i knew what i had to do but i knew not what i was doing. So I qualified for forgiveness. Hurray for me!

don't you see, goat, you can do whatever the fuck you want from monday to saturday night as long as you go to church on sunday and confess your sins because jesus loves you, that's what my old man said. and jesus loves to forgive …

they could've stopped me, understand. they had their chance. they could've stopped those who sinned before me, who sinned against me. they could've stopped what we do to each other. whoever they are. but they did not. because they were too busy doing unto others what others had done unto them.

i too had the golden rule to obey: do unto others as others have done onto you.

*   *   *

confession? is that what you want goat? it's what i have to do before i can forgive & be forgiven.

confess mother.

confess fucker.

confess father.

but sister? what have you to confess. your only crime, birth. for that you died.

How far the stars? she asks me one night as we sit under the lilac tree in the back yard exploring heaven's canopy.

how far the stars? she asks as she reaches towards them.

too far to reach, i tell her, except when you dream.

& she reaches her hands towards my face & places the palms of her hands over my eyes & she says, see. i can reach them.

OH GOD HOW I LOVED YOU LITTLE SISTER.

*   *   *

& that summer we're at the beach & i find a star-shaped sea shell. &when i give it to her i say: now you have your very own star. & she smiles & motions me towards her & kisses me on the cheek ... so petite & blonde & tiny ... & fair & innocent ...

& i wanted to say, i know he hurts you ... but i didn't know how to say it. & even if i knew how, what ... could ... .i do ... about it?

the potential for good & evil is in all of us, no?

so why did i choose to do what i did ...

i suffered the little children unto me ... No no no no no ... i made the little children suffer ...

i did it to them, the street urchins i attracted like flies.

i nailed them ...

three of them ...

to the crosses i had erected ...

in the basement of the home ...

in which i grew up ...

i hammered them ...

to my crosses ...

yes. i ZAP the channel changer. i walked the streets. i picked them out, cut them from the heard. i offered them sex drugs 'n rock 'n roll. & i snuffed them out. three of them.

father son & holy spirit.

i crucified them—innocents all—on the rugged crosses that i constructed in my abandoned home home on the range ...

yes, i confess. i knew not what i was doing to their naked bleeding broken bodies. i should've understood. i was old enough to understand. but, you see, i thought their screams were screams of ecstasy. because it felt good, what i did ...

how far the FUCKING stars??????

& they wept.

& they bled.

& they died.

& mother cried ...

when she broke into the bathroom.

but what she saw was never spoken of again.

& she remained silent until the day she died.

*　*　*

forgive me forgive me forgive me for i know not what i do even now as i confess before the temple vale is rent in two & i give up the ghost.

they wept & i laughed & i laughed as they wept.

& squatter's rights ended when i lit a match & created hell fire in the house where i grew up ...

if only they had never cut off my cable, i might have been able ...

*　*　*

& that is why i'm here, isn't it goat?

it has nothing to do with what daddy did or mother did. or with what we did to sister ...

it's because i did unto others what had been done unto me. & now you're going to crucify me.

there is no forgiveness, is there goat?

*   *   *

& the day segues into night. the night is long. it carries on. soon it will be dawn, again. my fourteen days will soon be done. but are my lessons done? are my lessons done?

to think, one time i could've been the champion copywriter of the world.

to think, she would've bore my baby.

to think, if it be thy will, soon i will think no more.

*   *   *

you are wrong, goat. confession is not good for the soul. this is not the first step to heeling the heel. already i know what i must do to make amends for what i have done. but who will avenge all that has been done to me and her and her too? & all that has been done, is being done, will be done? Done in His name? that too.

*   *   *

2nite there will be an accident, proving that the pen is mightier than the sword. for i have seen what i have done. & i know my sentence has begun.

2nite i will write thru these eyes that have seen what i have done & what has been done ... & i will write the final chapter on the screen behind my eyes.

i will write forever more. & forever more i will never more write again.

& the morning papers will scream my name in big bold type: Crucifier Crucified.

they will report that he fell on his pen & it pierced his eyes & distorted his brain.

perhaps i can make this all look like an accident.

an accident, yes. But oh dear, and accident and I am wearing soiled underwear. That will never do. Because mama said, change your dirty underwear. You want to wear clean underwear under there in case you have an accident ... how many nights, did I have jus that, accidents. accidents that soiled my underwear ... so many nights, accidents. I don't know how mama kept me in underwear ...

it's time for me to do what i should have done so long ago—curse a non-existent god & die. & if i am wrong, if there is god, then i will curse Almighty & happily take my place in hell. but if i am right, if there is no god, then i will curse the All-impotent & vacate this hell on earth. i will curse the void & be set free.

a simple accident & i will be set free. free to burn or turn to dust or feed the worms ... like mama and papa and little sister and the three cross urchins ... free to feed the worms ... but what if there is a god? Could it be that little sister is with the stars? Let it be, let it be. Let her be among the stars.

*　　*　　*

Jean Paul got this right: 'Hell is other people.' Amen to that. Which means goat, that other people have made my life hell. Hell on earth. But I too, goat, have been, to other people, the other people. I have been their hell.

But this he got wrong: 'No Exit.' There is an exit, goat. There is indeed an exit indeed in need I peed smoked weed gave into my greed for feed… the flesh I can exit; there is an exit, JP, indeed.

*　　*　　*

Feel free now to touch that dial. we won't be right back after this permanent interruption from our sponsor ...

Dogs, would you live forever? What more can i say? what more can i write? There is nothing I can right. I shall not see thee today goat, after all. I shall not. Bang bang.

hold my pen, mightier than the sword. fall upon my pen, to the end ... of hell on earth ... & expire with one final thrust & ...

... it is finish ...

EPILOGUE

I am not sure what to say, by way of conclusion, other than to clarify what may be seen as a logical conclusion on the reader's part, given the end of the Journal, as might be implied.

Simon P is not dead. He did not take his life on the last day of writing his journal.

It is unfortunate, the lives he took at the Lilac Hills Institute on the last day of writing his journal. It has still not been officially determined how he got into the maintenance room to get the hammer. Although it is most likely he killed the janitor first and took his key to get into the room. But autopsy reports revealed the janitor was killed by the hammer Simon removed from the room. So the jury is still out.

The class action lawsuits filed by the families of the patients, nurses, orderlies and staff at the institute have long been settled, although they continued filing suits that have delayed the publication of Simon's journal for over 20 years.

Simon has long ago been moved to a maximum security institution, against my recommendations after I read his journal. He was, I believe in my capacity as a professional psychiatrist, close, so close, to a major breakthrough.

In fact, I feel he experienced a major breakthrough, like the climax of a suspense novel. All that was missing was the dénouement—the self-reflection at the end of the work that puts it all, in this case a life, in perspective. And this is where I take full responsibility. Had I been reading the Journal, I may have intervened. I may have seen that climax had been achieved and intervened to guide Simon to a dénouement worthy of the work—the difficult work—that he had done over the time he spent in my company and in his room writing faithfully.

For that, I apologize. And note that the College of Psychologists of Canada has cleared my name, acknowledging that the experimental therapy had been peer reviewed and sanctioned with great enthusiasm and no dissenting voices. But the treatment, which I deem all but a success, was deemed a failure by the College and, as mentioned, is no longer sanctioned, even though I proposed modifications to the therapy, which I now use in my private practice, with result that have improved the psychological lives and well being of patients, although none are institutionalized nor have they demonstrated the tendencies demonstrated by Simon P.

I still believe the therapy can return humanity and dignity, understanding and clarity, self-compassion and self-esteem to a Simon P and others of his ilk. And I hope, one day, to put into practice intensive non-interventionist therapy with a patient as deserving, sadly so of course that one should be so deserving, as Simon P.

Dr. Heinrich Gautier

www.ingramcontent.com/pod-product-compliance
Lightning Source LLC
Chambersburg PA
CBHW070331260626
47160CB00003B/1011